NEW YORK REVIEW BOOKS
CLASSICS

MARSHLANDS

ANDRÉ GIDE (1869–1951) was born in Paris to a wealthy
Protestant family with Huguenot roots. His father, a prominent
law professor, died when Gide was still a child, and until well
into his teens the anxious and sickly boy was tutored at home
under the vigilant eye of his formidably pious mother. Gide
attended the salon of the symbolist poet Stéphane Mallarmé,
struck up a friendship with Oscar Wilde, and, at the age of
twenty-one, self-published his first book, *The Notebooks of André
Walter*. Visits to North Africa awakened the young man to his
homosexuality; summoned back from one of these trips in 1895
by his mother's death, he immediately married his deeply
religious cousin Madeleine Rondeaux, the beginning of an
intense, tortured, and sexually unconsummated relationship
that was central to Gide's life and work. A series of short fictions
exploring the relationship between faith and desire, *The Fruits
of the Earth*, *The Immoralist*, and *Strait Is the Gate*—none of
them enjoying popular success on publication—made Gide's
name as a writer, and as a founder of the journal *La Nouvelle
Revue Française* and a member of the editorial board of the
new publishing house Gallimard he became a central figure
not only in the French literary world but in the development
and promulgation of literary modernism around the world.
The Vatican Cellars, a picaresque tale in which the antihero
commits murder as a purely "gratuitous act," exercised a seminal
influence on surrealism and existentialism. *If It Die . . .*, Gide's
account of his childhood and coming-of-age and one of the first

memoirs to divulge the homosexuality of the author, was published at considerable legal risk in 1926. In the 1920s and '30s, Gide's reports on his visits to the Congo and the USSR served as controversial and effective exposés of the abuses of both French colonialism and Soviet Communism. In 1947, he received the Nobel Prize in Literature. Among the other notable works of this tirelessly industrious and enormously wide-ranging writer (he was also a gifted pianist, and regularly had a piano shipped to him on his travels) are *The Counterfeiters*, a novel, and the extraordinary *Journal* that he worked on from his teenage years until the end of his life.

DAMION SEARLS has translated eleven books for NYRB Classics, including Uwe Johnson's four-book novel *Anniversaries* (published in two volumes). This is his second translation of Gide's *Marshlands*; he also rewrote it as "56 Water Street," the first short story in his collection *What We Were Doing and Where We Were Going*.

DUBRAVKA UGRESIC is the author of seven works of fiction, including *The Museum of Unconditional Surrender* and *Baba Yaga Laid an Egg*, and six collections of essays. Her most recent book is *The Age of Skin: Essays*. In 2016 she received the Neustadt International Prize for Literature for her body of work.

MARSHLANDS

ANDRÉ GIDE

Translated from the French by
DAMION SEARLS

Preface by
DUBRAVKA UGRESIC

NEW YORK REVIEW BOOKS

New York

THIS IS A NEW YORK REVIEW BOOK
PUBLISHED BY THE NEW YORK REVIEW OF BOOKS
435 Hudson Street, New York, NY 10014
www.nyrb.com

This work received support from the French Ministry of Foreign Affairs and
the Cultural Services of the French Embassy in the United States through their
publishing assistance program.

First published by New York Review Books Classics in 2021.

Library of Congress Cataloging-in-Publication Data
Names: Gide, André, 1869–1951, author. | Searls, Damion, translator. |
    Ugrešić, Dubravka, writer of preface.
Title: Marshlands / by André Gide; translated by Damion Searls; [preface by
    Dubravka Ugresic].
Other titles: Paludes. English
Description: New York: New York Review Books, [2020] | Series: New York
    Review Books classics | Translated into English from French.
Identifiers: LCCN 2020016150 (print) | LCCN 2020016151 (ebook) |
    ISBN 9781681374727 (paperback) | ISBN 9781681374734 (ebook)
Classification: LCC PQ2613.I2 P313 2020 (print) | LCC PQ2613.I2 (ebook) |
    DDC 843/.912—dc23
LC record available at https://lccn.loc.gov/2020016150
LC ebook record available at https://lccn.loc.gov/2020016151

ISBN 978-1-68137-472-7
Available as an electronic book; ISBN 978-1-68137-473-4

Printed in the United States of America on acid-free paper.
10 9 8 7 6 5 4 3 2 1

CONTENTS

PREFACE

THICK books aren't the only ones with a literary destiny, slim books have one, too!

WHY A PREFACE?

Prefaces usually offer the reader a guide to the book before them; they say a few words about the book's author and place the book in its historical or contemporary literary context. In the pre-Internet age this was a job entrusted to literary experts. Today, with the assistance of the Internet, expertise is no longer considered necessary. I confess, I myself am no expert, or arbiter, or competent interpreter of Gide's work. I am here merely as a literary interloper and I see it as my task to respond to two questions:

1. How did this little French book come to be translated into English?

2. Why did I once love this book, do I love it still today, and if I have loved it, why do I think others will?

LITERATURE AS SEDUCTION

I made the acquaintance of Damion Searls—who has translated *Marshlands* into English—in 1998 at a literary event in Vienna. Our encounter was fleeting and superficial. Four years later, when he was on a Fulbright, Damion turned up in Amsterdam. This was our chance to spend more time together.

True booklovers—writers, critics, translators, publishers, and readers—can be identified (or at least I identify them!) by the way they allow themselves to be "seduced" by books. If the art of the word, meaning literature, is a form of inter-human communication, then "seduction" is one of the forms this communication takes. Literary seduction doesn't know or respect age, nor national, ethnic, racial, gender, or cultural boundaries. Yet finding a true friend, a booklover, is a true rarity.

In Isaac Babel's story "In the Basement," the narrator is a poor secondary-school student (the young Babel) from the Odessa Jewish ghetto who seeks to enchant Mark Borgman, a young man of his own age, by reciting Shakespeare to him, and in the end Shakespeare's verses serve as a smoke screen behind which Babel tries, and fails, to hide the penury, brutality, and tragicomedy of his real-life environment, so different from Borgman's.

Thrilled by the discovery that they share the same passions, booklovers, peacock-like, fan their verbal feathers. It just so happened that I mentioned *Marshlands* to Damion, and probably said along the way that it is my favorite book, which was certainly not true then, nor is it now. There is no *one single* favorite book for a bona fide lover of literature.

Be that as it may, I slipped the quote "Tityrus smiled" into *Pose for Prose*, my first book of stories, as if it were one of those ritual Christmas loafs or cakes with a ducat baked in it for good luck. There is also a line in *Lend Me Your*

Character, a collection of stories, that hints at my romance with *Marshlands*. Writers-booklovers aim to seduce their readers and listeners with books by other writers, the ones who seduced them as readers. Some among them will hide their literary "affairs" and eradicate all trace, while others will openly flaunt them, and yet others (ah, human frailty!) will fabricate theirs. Many aren't even aware of their literary "affairs." *The Attic*, a short novel by the Yugoslav writer Danilo Kiš, is strikingly reminiscent of *Marshlands*. Perhaps Kiš succumbed briefly to youthful literary transgressions and fell gloriously victim to literary seduction.

THE WORKERS' LIBRARY

There are many details I never would have recalled had I not come back to revisit this novel. I realized, for instance, that I don't have a copy of the actual book of *Marshlands* in my Amsterdam home library. Instead, what I found was a tattered photocopy of an age-old Yugoslav edition. The paper of the photocopy is coarse to the touch, you can't find this grade of paper anymore; the translation is awful, which only contributes to the charm that radiates from the little book; the stamp on the first page of the book shows it was borrowed from the Workers' Library in Zagreb. The Workers' Library, I should say, is long gone, as are workers, and workers' culture, nor is there any of the respect for workers which socialist society so earnestly promoted. Over many of the pages of the Yugoslav edition of *Marshlands* slinks the faded stamp of the Workers' Library, which, along with the text of *Marshlands* and the reader's sense of playfulness, gives an additional fillip to the read. This is particularly true of the dialogue between the narrator and his friends, which repeats several times and in several versions throughout the book ...

"So!" he said. "Hard at work?"
"I am writing *Marshlands*," I replied.
"What's that?"

                                        "A book."
"Will I like it?"

                                        "No."
"Too intellectual?"

                                        "Too boring."
"Why write it then?"

                                        "If I don't, who will?"
"I see, more personal confessions."

                                        "Hardly any."
"Well what's it about then?"

At the end of the book we find: "Table of the Most Remarkable Sentences in *Marshlands*." The list is very modest.

Page 9. "'So!' he said. 'Hard at work?'"
Page 80. "'Once you take up an idea, you have to carry it through to the end.'"

Then follows a page on which space has been left blank. It is meant for the reader. ("Given the prevalence of personal preferences, we leave the job of completing this page to each individual reader.") And here, in the empty space, denying readers the chance to introduce their own favorite sentence, an unknown librarian stamped the wavery Workers' Library stamp. And so it was that the anonymous librarian inadvertently added yet another possible interpretation to *Marshlands*.

Gide's *Marshlands* was published in 1895, while Goncharov's novel *Oblomov* came out in 1859. (Might this truncated numerical palindrome, 59/95, have brought the two books into some sort of "fateful" link?) *Marshlands* could be a short French version of the Russian *Oblomov*. Oblomov is a Russian nobleman, a person who prefers his bed to the challenges of real life. Gide's narrator in *Marshlands* is a writer whose qualms about writing persist for an unhealthily long time ("*Marshlands* is the story of someone who does not understand life, who writhes and worries for having believed in anything except the *one thing needful*"), leaving the reader to wonder whether this work is a small-scale French take on *Oblomov*.

Imagine for a moment an American edition of Marcel Proust through which sprints a stamp advertising Coca-Cola, or a Chinese edition of Walt Whitman through which creep the sayings of Mao Zedong. Whatever the case, the detail with the Workers' Library stamp is not why I have been carrying this tattered photocopy of *Marshlands* with me my whole life. As I have moved around the world I have left behind many important books. So why did this unsightly photocopy settle down in my Amsterdam library? I don't know, nor will I ever know.

As far as translator Damion Searls is concerned, apparently he chose as his favorite the sentence "Once you take up an idea, you have to carry it through to the end," by adding his translation of *Marshlands* to the long list of his published translations, nearly two decades after our conversation.

CANONICAL AND "WILD" LITERATURE

When I was first a student of comparative literature at the Faculty of Humanities and Social Science in Zagreb, *Marshlands* was one of my favorite books. The "ducats," the quotes I baked into my early books of prose, make that abundantly clear. Why wasn't I more prudent? With sharper intellectual acumen? I could have spiked my text with quotes from more respectable writers, like James Joyce, Vladimir Nabokov, or J. L. Borges. The last of these, Borges, was the fad of my literary generation, mainly among the boys. The boys dashed onto the pitch of the Croatian literature of the day as if they were a soccer team with J. L. Borges as their coach, and dubbed themselves the Croatian Borges Boys, drawing the attention of the literary community. Indeed, they played in one or two lackluster literary championships and then quickly succumbed to the domestic variety of commercial genre literature. At the time (in the 1970s), among the various Yugoslav cultural centers, at least as far as literary taste and trends go, the differences were far greater then than they are now, postwar, when the writers' communities are part of entirely separate, distinct countries. The globalized literary marketplace tends to homogenize literary taste, and in this, by and large, it succeeds.

The Belgrade literary world, or at least one small part of it, developed a taste at one time for outlandish characters and narrators, for outsiders, malcontents on the fringes of society, "fools," "wild people." The filmmaker Dušan Makavejev dedicated his movie *Innocence Unprotected* (1968) to Dragoljub

Aleksić, a gymnast who made a movie about himself at the beginning of World War II. The narrator of the novel *My Family's Role in the World Revolution* (1969) by Bora Ćosić is a young boy who looks at the world around him with the disconcerting eyes of a child. Milovan Danojlić wrote *Kako je Dobrislav protrčao kroz Jugoslaviju* (How Dobrislav Ran Across Yugoslavia, 1977) about an amateur writer who travels through Yugoslavia, selling his amateur books. Not only is the novel filled with touching sympathy for "colleagues," it blurs the lines between "established" and "unestablished" writers. Moma Dimić wrote *Šumski građanin* (Forest Citizen), a documentary novel about a similar protagonist, a flesh-and-blood person, an outsider, a renegade, a "fool," while the cult Yugoslav film director Slobodan Šijan made the film *How I Was Systematically Destroyed by an Idiot* (1983) based on Dimić's novel. Only at a time such as this could Stanoje Ćebić, a metalworker by training, author of the book *Zašto sam postao vo* (Why I Became an Ox), become a media star, albeit briefly. Ćebić also appeared in *Kolt 15 GAP*, a unique documentary about himself.

Today, the atmosphere that existed in the individual cultural circles of those days is difficult to access and all but defies translation, even in the very locations where it ruled. If the "cultural products" of those years haven't been completely consigned to oblivion as nonrepresentative, at least they have been sidelined to the niche of cultural excess. Reception for "outlandish" protagonists and their authentic voices was not a cynical pastime of the privileged in culture; instead, it was an assault on the canon, on the personalities of the authors who had been enthroned as the "fathers," the omniscient moral, intellectual, and aesthetic arbiters, the writers of pompous national works with pompous literary heroes, thereby constructing an unwritten literary norm. This was, of course, a blow to the authority of the then ruling aesthetic values by rendering them ridiculous. So there you have it: *Marshlands*, the book André Gide himself described as a *sotie*, resonated with my newly awakened aesthetic receptiveness for the minor, the fringe, the anticanonic, the outsider, and the subversive.

Why am I bothering the reader with obscure data from a literary provincial backwater? But doesn't *Marshlands* itself come to the American market from the obscure backwaters of Europe? There isn't just one reader out there in the world. Among readers there are those intrigued by obscure data. These details expose a hidden dynamic within the national literatures, which is of little interest to those penning national literary histories. These details furthermore disclose the ways books travel through the world literary field. World literature doesn't always move along the regular routes anointed books travel from point A to point B. World literature also exists thanks in part to the chaos of traffic when one travels to New York via Baghdad, Barcelona (not the one in Spain, but the one in Venezuela!), Singapore, and Kiev...True, there is more traffic today than ever, so books from Barangaroo find their way to New York, yet at the same time the pathways are more "set" in terms of traffic; the mighty literary marketplace plays the role of literary traffic control. This is why, right now in Barcelona, Singapore, Kiev, and New York, readers are reading the same titles, which have been translated into the local languages. This "totalitarian" constellation is being sabotaged by booklovers, bookworms. Led by their passion for books, writers, translators, readers, editors, and the many others who take part in this act of literary sabotage tunnel their way using secret underground passageways, excavate displaced values, dust off forgotten books. Their passion is their mission.

CHARM AND HOW TO COME BY IT

André Gide is one of the preeminent authors of European modernism. He was a prolific writer, whose novels (*The Immoralist, The Counterfeiters, The Vatican Cellars* or *Lafcadio's Adventures, The Pastoral Symphony*) and many other texts are firmly built into the canon of French and world literature. And the fact that Gide's varied opus was honored by the Nobel Prize in Literature in 1947 also figures into this.

Yet *Marshlands* seems to have broken away from Gide's significant literary opus. Maybe the author himself pushed *Marshlands* to break away by describing it as a *sotie*, the old carnival genre, a street-fair farce, a Feast of Fools. We should add that *Marshlands* is not the only *sotie* Gide wrote. The brief description that qualifies *Marshlands* as a satire of Parisian salon literary life at the turn of the nineteenth to the twentieth century is not entirely inaccurate.

But *Marshlands* is more than that.

It is a book that broke away, in a sense, from the opus of its author. We could easily proclaim *Marshlands* a genre-bending book and add it to the family of slim satirical novels about artists, which were published later, whether or not they were inspired by Gide. Two of these, for instance, are *The Works and Days of Svistonov* (1929) by Konstantin Vaginov and *Life and Work of the Composer Foltýn* (1939) by Karel Čapek. In all of them dwells Tityrus, who "sits careless in the shade."

Yet *Marshlands* is more than that.

I'm guessing that André Gide didn't stop to think whether *Marshlands* would outlive him. This is a role he'd intended for his other, more important books. It would be hard to imagine that this slim volume could become Gide's trademark work. The possibility for this, however, remains open. For, who knows, maybe with *Marshlands* Gide laid the explosives under his canonic work, so others would do so after his death. ("I like every book to include its own refutation, but hidden. It should not sit atop its idea, afraid to look it in the face. I like it to include what denies it, to self-destruct.")

Yet *Marshlands* is so much more than that.

Some books travel, others stay in place. Some end up coated in the dust of oblivion, others are always read and reread, though despite this they remain snared in their time like flies in amber. Then there are the rare breakaway books that abandon their author, home, context, time, books with wanderlust that slip almost illegally across borders, move from place to place, from one random reader to another. What is it in them that makes them so eternally appealing? Wherein lies the secret of their stamina? Why can *Marshlands* so readily be seen as an exemplar of literary postmodernism? And while we might find some acclaimed contemporary writers easy to place in the nineteenth century, not so much, perhaps, by what they have chosen to write about as by the way they went about the writing, *Marshlands* is a surprisingly youthful book. If we were to assign another author's name to it and claim it was the debut novel of one of our contemporaries, few readers would spot the switch.

No, *Marshlands* is more than that.

What sets *Marshlands* apart from so many other books is the elusive quality it has, something novels (and people) rarely possess. That quality is charm. Some books seduce us with their importance, others with their pomposity, yet others with their impressive reach, or tense narration, or pertinence. Every author knows, or seems to know, which of these is his or her *strength*. Readers know, or seem to know, their literary tastes.

So what would literary charm be?

Reading *Marshlands* again, after so many years, I was reminded of another book that erased its author and his intentions to remain inscribed in the history of literature as a "serious" author. The author is A. A. Milne, and his masterpieces are *Winnie-the-Pooh* and *The House at Pooh Corner*. Quite possibly, the literary destiny of an exceptional book derives from a mistake. ("No one seems to understand that, having done a thing, what one wants is precisely to do something else.") Although Milne's book clearly is written for children, its most numerous and devoted readers are adult booklovers. Hamlet? Raskolnikov? Leopold Bloom? Where on the list of celebrated literary characters can we find Eeyore?! Eeyore, the woeful donkey from *Winnie-the-Pooh*, is one of my favorite literary figures. Eeyore ends up tailless and homeless. Eeyore is an outcast, a skeptic, a would-be philosopher, a grouch (or a loser, as we'd say today). Eeyore is a serious literary character whose tears touch the readers' empathy and spark laughter. The narrator of *Marshlands* is a woeful writer (a loser, as we'd say today) who keeps a diary of his life (or, better said, his absence of a life) and works on his novel, which also happens to have the title *Marshlands*. The friends who surround him are reminiscent of Milne's stuffed-animal characters, and the narrator of *Marshlands* is strikingly reminiscent of Eeyore. ("We are an indefinite mix of laughter and melancholy, like a partly cloudy day. Having cried just once, our laughter is not believed; having joked just once, we are no longer taken seriously."

But, nevertheless, isn't *Marshlands* more than that?

To be honest, I don't know. But I do know that now is the time for me to retreat. I realize that by seeking the same sort of literary attention for the character of Raskolnikov as for the characters of the self-named writer in *Marshlands* and Eeyore in all his plushness, I am undermining the established hierarchy and raising questions about my own literary credibility. In other words, I'm sawing through the branch I'm sitting on. So now it's up to you, dear reader, to negotiate this for yourself and judge whether or not the literary coordinates I have offered can be of help. Happy reading!

—DUBRAVKA UGRESIC
Translated by Ellen Elias-Bursac

TRANSLATOR'S NOTE

GEORGE D. Painter's 1953 translation of *Marshlands* is dedicated to Dorothy Bussy, "Gide's incomparable translator and friend." I dedicate the present translation to Painter, in whose version I first read and loved Gide's *Marshlands*, and from whom I have taken some phrases. His rendering of Gide's title *Paludes* is unimprovable.

Painter's translation also, from today's perspective, turns Gide's somewhat campy French into very campy British English. While I have not gone in whole hog for anachronism—translating the characters' constant interjections of "*Monsieur!*" with, for instance, "Dude!"—I have made them speak in my language, which is American English. The French "*Tiens! Tu travailles?*"—Painter's "I say! Are you writing?"—I translate as "So! Hard at work?" (The actual spoken American English might be: "Hey. Busy?")

Gide published *Paludes* in 1895 and in three later editions (1896, 1920, 1932), each with slight revisions. In November 1895, Gide published a "Preface for a Second Edition of *Marshlands*," which was included in the 1896 edition under the title "Afterword to the New Edition of *Marshlands* and an Announcement of the Forthcoming Book *The Fruits of the Earth*." Gide made the most changes to the 1920 edition, notably removing the book's subtitle, "Treatise on Contingency"; re-removing the afterword; and cutting three episodes that probably seemed, at twenty-five years' distance, too specific to the 1890s Parisian symbolist scene. A note in the 2009 Pléiade edition of Gide's collected fiction says, rightly, that *Marshlands* is at once his most dated work and his most timeless—and by 1920, Gide was emphasizing the latter.

The present volume translates the final, 1932 edition. It also includes two related poems, the three deleted scenes, and the "Preface for a Second Edition." Gide's later book *Prometheus Misbound* (1899), in which Prometheus, Zeus, and the eagle gallivant around Paris, was also translated by Painter and published together with *Marshlands* in 1953: it contains a chapter in which Prometheus tells "The Story of Tityrus," which is translated here as well.

Translations of Latin words and phrases are given at the end of the book.

MARSHLANDS

This satire of...what?
was written for my friend
Eugène Rouart

Dic cur hic.

(The other school of thought)

Before I explain my book to people, I am waiting for people to explain it to me. Explaining something up front only limits its meaning anyway, for even assuming that we know what we want to say, we don't know if that is all we actually will say. —One always says more than just THAT. —What I am most interested in is the part I put in without knowing it: the unconscious part, or as I would say, the part from God.

A book is always a collaboration, and the better it is, the smaller the writer's share in it and the more it is able to welcome God into it.

Always and everywhere, we await the revelation of things; from the public, we await the revelation of our own works.

HUBERT

AROUND five o'clock, it started to get cold outside; I closed my windows and returned to my writing.

At six o'clock, my dear friend Hubert walked in. He was back from riding school.

"So!" he said. "Hard at work?"

"I am writing *Marshlands*," I replied.

"What's that?"

                                        "A book."

"Will I like it?"

                                        "No."

"Too intellectual?"

                                        "Too boring."

"Why write it then?"

                                        "If I don't, who will?"

"I see, more personal confessions."

                                        "Hardly any."

"Well what's it about then?"

                                        "Sit down, I'll tell you."

When he did, I said:

"I read these two lines in Virgil:

Et tibi magna satis quamvis lapis omnia nudus
Limosoque palus obducat pascua junco.

"Translation: There's a shepherd talking to another shepherd, and he tells him his field may be stony and swampy but it's good enough for him, and being satisfied with it makes him very happy. —There is no wiser thought than that, if you are unable to change your field, don't you think?"

Hubert said nothing. I went on: "*Marshlands*, then, is the story of someone who cannot travel. I shall call him Tityrus, after Virgil. *Marshlands* is the story of a man who, possessing the field of Tityrus, does not strive to leave it, but rather contents himself with it. There you have it.

"Here is the plot: On the first day, he realizes that he is content, and wonders what he should do. On the second day, a ship passes by, he kills four birds in the morning—scoters, or teals—and as evening approaches he eats two of them, cooked over a humble fire he has made from sticks and shrubs. On the third day, he amuses himself building a hut out of long reeds. On the fourth day, he eats the other two scoters. On the fifth day, he takes apart his hut and gets to work building a more complicated house. On the sixth day, . . ."

"Enough!" Hubert said. "I get it. —You certainly know how to write, my dear friend." He left.

By then it was night. I arranged my papers. I did not eat dinner; I went out and got to Angela's apartment around eight o'clock.

Angela was still at the table, eating a little fruit for her dessert. I sat down next to her and started to peel her an orange. The maid brought in some jam and, after we were alone again, Angela made me a tartine and said:

"What did you do today?"

I could not remember one single thing I had done, so I said, rather rudely: "Nothing." But then, anxious to avoid psychological digressions, I remembered my visitor and exclaimed: "My dear friend Hubert came to see me at six o'clock!"

"He's just left," Angela said. Then, returning once again to the subject of an old argument between us, she said: "At least he does something. He's very busy."

I had already said that I hadn't done anything, so this made me angry. "What do you mean? What does he do?" I asked. And she was off:

"All sorts of things... First of all, he rides horses, and then, as you know perfectly well, he is on the board of directors of four major companies, and he and his brother-in-law run another, hailstorm insurance—which reminds me, I need to get a policy. He takes adult education courses in biology and gives public readings every Tuesday night. He knows enough medicine to come in handy if there's ever an accident. Hubert does lots of good works: five destitute families owe him their continued subsistence; he brings workers lacking work and bosses lacking workers together. He sends scrawny children out to the country, where there are institutions for their recuperation. He founded a wickerwork studio to employ the young blind, I mean, the blind young... And you! What do you do?"

"Me!" I answered, a bit ashamed. "I am writing *Marshlands*."

"*Marshlands*, what's that?" she said.

We finished eating and I waited until we were in the living room before I replied. Then, when we were seated by the fireplace, I began:

"*Marshlands* is the story of a bachelor living in a tower surrounded by marshes."

"Oh!" she cried.

"His name is Tityrus."

"Awful name."

"Not at all," I shot back, "it's from Virgil. Besides, I never make things up."

"Why a bachelor?"

"Oh, it just makes it simpler."

"That's it?"

"No, I tell the story of what he does."

"And what does he do?"

"He looks at the scoters."

After a long silence, she said: "Why do you write these books of yours?"

"Why? I don't know... Probably to have something to do."

"Read it to me," Angela said.

"If you insist. I have precisely four or five pages of it here in my pocket." Taking them out, I read to her as listlessly and monotonously as I could:

"TITYRUS'S JOURNAL,
or MARSHLANDS

"From my window, when I raise my head slightly, I see a garden I have never really looked at closely; to the right, a tree shedding its leaves; past the garden, the plains; to the left, a lake about which I will soon have something more to say.

"Ages ago, someone planted hollyhocks and columbines in the garden, but I have neglected them and let the plants run wild. Because of the neighboring pond, rushes and moss have swallowed everything; the paths have vanished beneath the grass; there is nowhere left I can

walk except the long footpath leading from my chamber
to the plains: the path I took one day when I decided to
take a stroll. At night, the forest creatures cross it to go
drink from the lake; in the twilight I can only just make
out the gray shapes, and since night falls soon afterward,
I never see them coming back."

"Ooh, that would be scary," Angela said. "But do go on,
it's very well written."

The effort it took to read these pages had made me very
tense.

"Oh, that's almost everything," I told her. "The rest isn't
done yet."

"Notes!" she cried. "Oh, read them! Those are always so
interesting, you can see what the writer is trying to say much
better from notes than from what he writes afterward."

This was rather disappointing, but oh well. I went on,
trying to give the sentences an unfinished ring:

"*Tityrus can fish from the windows in his tower,* ... I told
you, these are just rough notes ..."

"Do keep going!"

"*The dreariness, of waiting for the fish; not enough bait;*
more and more lines (symbolic); the inevitability of his not
catching anything."

"Why?"

"It's a symbolic truth."

"But what if he did catch something?"

"Then that would be a different symbol, and a different
truth."

"But it's not about truth, you can change the facts to make
them be whatever you want."

"I arrange the facts to make them conform to the truth

more closely than they do in real life. I can't explain it to you now, it's too complicated. But the thing is to believe that the events are appropriate to the characters—that's what makes a good novel, the conviction that nothing that happens to anyone fits anyone else. Hubert would already have had a miraculous catch! Tityrus doesn't catch a thing. It's a psychological truth."

"All right. Go ahead."

"*The moss on the riverbank, extending out under the water. The indecision of reflections. Algae. Fish go by. In describing them, avoid at all costs the phrase 'opaque stupor.'*"

"I should hope so! Why even put that note in?"

"Because my friend Hermogène has already used that phrase to describe carp."

"I don't think it's a good term at all."

"I'm sorry you think so. Should I keep going?"

"Please. These notes of yours are very entertaining."

"*Tityrus, at dawn, sees white cones rising from the plain—saltworks. He goes down to watch the men work. —Nonexistent landscape; narrow dikes running between two salt marshes. Pyramids of salt, white, too white (symbol). You can't look right at them unless it's foggy. Tinted eyeglasses protect the workers from ophthalmia.*

"*Tityrus puts a handful of salt in his pocket, then returns to his tower. —*That's it."

"That's it?"

"That's all I've written so far."

"I'm afraid this story of yours might be the least little bit boring," Angela said.

A vastness of silence—subsequent to which I cried, my voice full of feeling: "Angela, Angela, please! When will you understand what books are about? What I'm trying to express is the emotion I get from my life: boredom, vanity, monotony. It doesn't matter to me, because I am writing *Marshlands*, but Tityrus's life is empty, nothing. And as for you and me, Angela, I promise you, our own prospects are even duller and more mediocre."

"That's not how I feel about it," Angela said.

"That's because you don't think about it. Precisely the subject of my book! Tityrus is not unhappy with his life, he likes contemplating the marshes, the changes in the weather impart to them a pleasant variety. But look at yourself, look at your own story! How much variety do you find there?

"How long have you lived in this apartment? I know, low rent. Low rent! —And it's not just you! These windows, looking out on the street, or on backyards, and looking out you see walls or other people looking back at you . . . Must I go on? Your dresses, must I make you ashamed of them, too? And do you think we have ever really loved each other?"

"Nine o'clock," she said. "I have to go. Hubert is giving his reading tonight."

"What is he reading?" I asked, in spite of myself.

"Not *Marshlands*, that's for sure!" And she left.

Back home, I attempted to put the opening of *Marshlands* into verse. I wrote the first quatrain:

> *When I slightly raise my head,*
> *I from my window see*
> *The edge of a pretty little wood*
> *Where there's néver been féstivitý.*

And then I went to bed. My day was complete.

ANGELA

Wednesday

To KEEP a daily planner and write down what I need to do during the week, for every day: that is using one's time wisely. You decide your actions for yourself; having resolved upon them in advance, at your leisure, you are certain of not being dependent on the weather every morning. I draw up from my daily planner the sentiment of duty: I write in it a week in advance, so that I have time to forget what I wrote; surprises are always lying in wait, which are indispensable, given my way of life. I go to sleep every night facing a day to come that is unknown and nonetheless predetermined by me.

There are two sections of my daily planner: on one page, I write what I am going to do, and on the facing page, every night, I write what I've done. Then I compare the two, I subtract, and what I have not done, the deficit, becomes what I should have done, which I copy into the month of December, thereby generating various moral ideas in my spirit. —I started three days ago. —So this morning, opposite the directive "Try to get up at six," I wrote: "Got up at seven" and then, in parentheses, "(negative unforeseen)." Various other agenda items followed:

Write to Gustave and Léon.

Be stunned at not having received a letter from Jules.

Go see Gontran.

Think about Richard's personality.

Worry about the relationship between Hubert and Angela.

Try to make time to go to the Jardin des Plantes, to study the varieties of the lesser potamogeton, for *Marshlands*.

Spend the evening at Angela's.

Then came the following thought (I write down one thought a day, in advance, and it determines whether I am to be sad or joyous): "There are things one does anew each day simply because one has nothing better to do: there is no progress, there is not even staying in place, but after all one cannot do nothing… This is the same, in time, as the movement in space of caged wild animals or the tides on the beach."

I remembered that this idea came to me as I was walking past the outdoor tables of a restaurant and saw the waiters serving and clearing the plates.

I wrote underneath: "Good for *Marshlands*." And I started preparing to think about Richard's personality. I keep my reflections and repercussions on my best friends in a little writing desk, one drawer for each. I took out the bundle of notes and reread the following:

RICHARD

Sheet I.

An excellent man. I have great respect for him, and he deserves it.

Sheet II.

By dint of endless hard work, has managed to escape

the great misery into which he was plunged by the death of his parents. His grandmother is still alive; he wreathes her in the pious and affectionate care that one so often gives to the old. Some years ago, though, she entered her second childhood. He married a woman with less money than him, out of virtue, and his fidelity makes her happy. —Four children. I am the godfather of one of his little girls, who limps.

Sheet III.

Richard admired my father to a truly great extent. He is the most loyal of all my friends. He thinks he knows me perfectly, even though he has never read anything I've written. That is what makes it possible for me to write *Marshlands*. When I think of Tityrus, I think of him. I wish I had never met him.

He and Angela haven't met; they wouldn't understand each other.

Sheet IV.

I have the misfortune of being admired greatly by Richard—that is the reason why I never dare do anything. It is not easy to free oneself from another's admiration, as long as one continues to admire him in turn. Richard often tells me, with real feeling, that I am incapable of acting badly, and this restrains me when, as does occasionally happen, I am inclined to decide to do something. Richard values in me the passivity that keeps me on the paths of virtue, the paths onto which others like him have pushed me. He often calls it a virtue to accept one's lot, since that is a virtue the poor may practice.

Sheet V.

Works at an office all day, sits at his wife's side at night, reading the paper, so as to have something to talk about. "Have you seen the new Pailleron play at the Comédie Française?" he asked me. He always keeps up to date on the latest thing. "Are you going to go see the new gorillas?" he asked me, when he heard I was going to the Jardin des Plantes. Richard treats me like an overgrown child, I hate that. He doesn't take seriously what I do. I will tell him the story of *Marshlands*.

Sheet VI.

His wife's name is Ursula.

I took out a Sheet VII, and wrote:

Any career that brings in no profit is horrible—that brings in nothing but money, and so little that you have to start work over again without stopping. Stagnations! When people like that reach the moment of their death, what will they have done with their lives? They will have filled their allotted place. —I should think so! The place they will have occupied is as small as they are.

It doesn't matter to me, because I am writing *Marshlands*, but otherwise I would consider myself one of them. One really must try to vary one's existence a little.

Just then, my servant brought in a bite to eat and my letters: one from Jules, of all people, and I ceased to be stunned at his silence. I weighed myself, for my health, as I do every morning; I wrote a few lines to Léon, and to Gustave; then, while drinking my daily bowl of milk (the custom of certain of the Lake Poets), I thought: Hubert did not understand a thing about *Marshlands*; he cannot accept that an author, writing not to instruct, may still not be writing to entertain. Tityrus bores him. He does not understand any condition that isn't social. He thinks that because he is busy he has nothing in common with Tityrus—I must have explained myself badly. He thinks that everything has worked out because Tityrus is happy, but it is precisely because Tityrus is happy that I wish not to be. On the contrary. Get mad! I will make Tityrus contemptible, with his resignation...

I was about to start thinking about Richard's personality again when I heard the doorbell ring and the man himself, after sending in his card, walked in. I was slightly annoyed, since I cannot think about people very well when they are actually there.

"Ah, my dear friend!" I cried, embracing him. "What a coincidence! I was just going to think about you this morning."

"I've come to ask you a favor," he said. "Oh, it's practically nothing, but seeing as you don't have anything to do, I thought you could give me a moment of your time—it's just a simple signature, you only need to be there, I need a sponsor and you can vouch for me—I'll explain everything on the way, we have to hurry, I have to be at the office by ten o'clock."

I hate to seem idle, so I replied: "Luckily it's not even nine, we have time, but I have something to do myself right afterward at the Jardin des Plantes."

"Aha!" he began. "You are going to see the new—"

"No, my dear Richard," I interrupted, as it were smoothly, "not the new gorillas. I have to go study several varieties of the lesser potamogeton there, for *Marshlands*."

My idiotic answer immediately made me mad at Richard. He said nothing, afraid of seeming or making me seem ignorant. I thought: He should burst out laughing. But he doesn't dare to. I can't stand his pity. He obviously thinks I'm ridiculous. He keeps his feelings hidden to prevent my having to reveal to him that I feel the same way about him. But we both know we have these feelings. Our reciprocal respect survives because his leans against mine while mine rests on his; he doesn't dare take his away because he's afraid mine will collapse. He's so patronizingly nice to me . . . Huh! Never mind. I will tell him the story of *Marshlands* . . .

I began gently: "How's your wife?"

At once, Richard told me his own story, all by himself: "Ursula? Ah! The poor dear! Now it's her eyes, with eyestrain—and it's her own fault—can I tell you, dear friend, what I would never tell anyone else? I know I can trust your discretion. Here's the whole story: Edward, my brother-in-law, was in great need of money; it had to be found somehow. Ursula knew everything because Jeanne, her sister-in-law, had come to see her the same day. We were broke, we had had to put a stop to Albert's violin lessons to pay the cook, which made me sad, because they were Albert's only distraction during his long convalescence. The cook got wind of it somehow, I don't know how; the poor girl is very devoted to us—Louise, you know her. She came to see us in tears, saying she would rather not eat than deprive little Albert. We had to accept, so as not to offend the brave girl, but I decided to get up and work for two hours every night, while my wife thought I was asleep, and earn the money we were keeping from dear Louise with some translations of articles from English that I knew where I could publish.

"The first night, all was well. Ursula slept like a baby. The second night, no sooner had I started working than who did I see walk into the room? Ursula! She had had the same idea! She was making some little fireplace screens, which she knew where she could place—you know she has a gift for watercolors; they're adorable things, my friend—so she could pay Louise. We were both very moved, and tearfully embraced. In vain did I try to persuade her to go back to bed—she gets tired so easily—she absolutely refused—she begged me to let her work next to me, as the greatest possible proof of my affection for her; I had no choice but to let her. But she is getting so tired. That's what we do every night. It makes the following day a bit hard; in any case, we've decided there's no reason to go to bed in the first place now that we're not hiding it from each other."

"Richard! My goodness! This story you're telling me is exceedingly touching!" I cried, and thought: "No, I will never be able to tell him about *Marshlands*, not a chance," and murmured: "My dear Richard, please believe me when I say that I understand your sorrows very well. You are truly very unhappy."

"No, my friend," he said, "I am not unhappy. I have not been given many things in life, but those few things have been enough to make me happy. Do you think I told you this story to make you pity me? —Surrounded by love and respect, working next to my Ursula every night . . . I wouldn't exchange these pleasures for . . ."

A rather long silence ensued. Then I asked: "And the children?"

"Ah, the poor children!" he said. "That is what saddens me. They need fresh air, they need to play in the sun; too much time in cramped little rooms makes a child pale and sickly. I don't mind—I am old—I have accepted these things—

but my children, they are not happy, and that makes me suffer."

"It's true," I said, "your rooms are a bit musty...Then again, opening one's windows too wide simply lets in all the street smells...Well, there's always the Jardin du Luxembourg. That is precisely the subject of..." But at once I thought: No, I definitely cannot tell him about *Marshlands*—and I ended my aside by seeming to fall into deep contemplation.

After a little while, I was desperate enough to ask him for news of his grandmother, when Richard signaled that we had arrived.

"Hubert's already here," he said. "I haven't explained anything to you, have I...I need two cosigners—never mind— you know—it's all in the documents.

"I believe you've already met," Richard added, as I shook my great friend's hand. He started right in: "So! How goes *Marshlands*?"

I gripped his hand tighter and said in a low voice: "Shh! Not now! After we're done here we'll go somewhere we can talk."

And after signing the papers and saying goodbye to Richard, Hubert and I headed off. He, too, was walking in the direction of the Jardin des Plantes—he had a practicum in obstetrics to attend.

"So," I began, "here's the latest. You remember the scoters. Tityrus had killed four. As I said. But no! He can't: No hunting allowed. Suddenly a priest comes up and tells Tityrus that the Church would have been sad indeed to see him, Tityrus, eating teals; it is forbidden fruit, or rather forbidden game; one cannot be too careful; sin lies in wait for us everywhere; when in doubt, choose abstinence; it is better to mortify the flesh; the Church knows some excellent means of doing so, that have been proved effective. May I venture to offer advice to a fellow brother? Eat earthworms.

"As soon as the priest leaves, a doctor approaches. You were going to eat teal! Don't you know how dangerous that is? You have to watch out for malignant fevers in these marshes—your blood has to adapt—*similia similibus*, Tityrus! Eat bloodworms (*Lumbriculus limosus*) the essence of the marsh is concentrated in them. Plus they're very nutritious."

"Blegh!" Hubert uttered.

"I know, right? And the whole thing is a lie—as I'm sure you've figured out, they were only trying to preserve the game! But the most amazing thing is that Tityrus tries it, and gets used to the bloodworms after a few days, and in fact before long he will find them delicious. —Now tell me, isn't Tityrus disgusting!?"

"He is blessed," Hubert said.

"Well, let's change the subject," I cried, rather irritated now. And, suddenly remembering that I was supposed to worry about the relationship between Hubert and Angela, I tried to get him to talk:

"How monotonous it all is!" I began again, after a silence. "Nothing ever happens! —One simply must try to whip a little variety into one's life. But it's impossible to invent a passion where there isn't any! And besides, I don't know anyone except Angela—and she and I have never loved each other in a truly decisive way: anything I say to her tonight I might just as well have said to her the night before, there's no progress..."

I paused after each phrase, waiting. He said nothing. So, I mechanically continued: "It doesn't matter to me, because I am writing *Marshlands*—but what I can't stand is that she doesn't grasp the situation. In fact, that is what gave me the idea of writing *Marshlands*."

Finally, Hubert was moved to speak: "Why do you want to upset her if she's happy how she is?"

"But she isn't happy, my friend! She *thinks* she is, because she is unaware of her condition; you must admit, to be blind as well as average makes it that much more pathetic."

"And if you open her eyes, succeed in making her unhappy?"

"That would be much more interesting, for a start. At least she would no longer be satisfied—she would be searching…" But I could not find out anything more, for just then Hubert shrugged his shoulders and fell silent.

After a moment, he spoke again: "I didn't know you knew Richard."

It was almost a question. I could have told him that Richard was Tityrus. But, since Hubert had no right to despise Richard as far as I knew, I merely said: "I have great respect for him." And I promised myself I would make up for it by talking to Angela about him tonight.

"Well, goodbye," Hubert said, realizing our conversation was at an end. "I'm in a hurry, you walk too slow. —By the way, I can't come see you this evening at six o'clock."

"That's fine," I said. "It will be a change for us both."

He left. I walked into the botanical garden alone and slowly made my way to the plants. I love this place: I come here often, all the gardeners know me, they unlock the collections closed to the public and let me in, thinking I'm a scientist because I sit down by the ponds. Under the staff's constant supervision, these ponds remain in a natural state. A stream of water feeds into them; the plants that are allowed to grow there grow; many insects swim there. I spend my time watching them: that, in a way, is what gave me the idea of writing *Marshlands*: the feeling of useless contemplation, the emotion I get when faced with delicate gray things.

That day, I wrote for Tityrus:

Wide, flat landscapes attract me more than any others—monotonous moors—I would travel far to find a lake country, were it not that one surrounds me here.

Do not think from this that I am sad; I am not even melancholy, I am Tityrus, and a recluse, and I love landscapes, like books, that do not distract me from my own thoughts. For my thoughts are sad and serious and, even when other people are near, gloomy; I like my thoughts more than anything, and I especially seek out plains, unsmiling lakes, and moors because I can wander with them there. I wander gently with them.

Why are my thoughts sad? If I had been bothered by that fact, I would have asked myself that question more often. If you hadn't pointed it out to me, I might not have realized it myself, for often enough my thoughts delight in things you care absolutely nothing about. For instance, they like rereading these lines; they enjoy all the petty tasks it is useless to tell you about because you would not even recognize them ...

An almost-warm breeze was blowing. Frail grasses leaned over the water, bent with the weight of insects. Germinative thrusts pushed asunder the margins of the flagstones; a little water escaped and moistened the roots. Mosses reaching all the way to the bottom of the pond gave it depth with their shadow; glaucous pondweed held bubbles of air for larvae to breathe. A water beetle moved past. I could not hold back a poetic thought, and, taking a new sheet of paper out of my pocket, I wrote:

Tityrus smiled.

After which I felt hungry, so, putting off the potamogetons for another day, I went looking for the restaurant along the quay that Pierre had told me about. I wanted to be alone, but I saw Léon there, who spoke to me of Edgar. After lunch I went to see various men of letters. Around five o'clock, a light rain started to fall; I went back home; I wrote down definitions of twenty scholastic terms and thought up no fewer than eight new epithets for *blastoderm*.

By evening I was a little worn out, and, after dinner, I went to sleep at Angela's. At, not with: I have never done anything with her except harmless little substitutes.

She was alone. When I walked in, she was playing a Mozart sonatina with great precision on a freshly tuned piano. It was already late, and no other sound could be heard. She had lit all the candles in the candelabras and was wearing a dress with a small checked pattern.

"Angela," I said, walking in, "we should try to get a little variety into our lives! Are you going to ask me again what I did today?"

She obviously failed to grasp the bitterness of my words, because she asked me at once: "All right, what did you do today?"

To which, and in spite of myself, I answered: "I saw my great friend Hubert."

"He just left," Angela said.

"Really, Angela, can't you ever have us both here at the same time?" I cried.

"Maybe he doesn't especially want to do that," she said. "But if you're so keen on it, come over for dinner on Friday, he'll be here. You can read us some poetry... Speaking of which—tomorrow night. Did I invite you already? I'm having some men of letters over; you are one of them. It starts at nine."

"I saw several today," I replied, by which I meant literati. "How I love their tranquil lives. They are always busy working and yet you never bother them; when you go to see them, it is as if they were working only for you and that they would rather talk to you instead. Their polite remarks are so charming, they have had so much time to think them out. I like people whose lives are always full but can still be filled with us. And since everything they do is worthless anyway, you don't feel bad taking up their time. Speaking of which: I saw Tityrus."

"The bachelor?"

"Yes. In reality, though, he's married, the father of four. His name is Richard... And don't tell me he's just left too! You two haven't met."

Angela, somewhat hurt, said: "See, your story isn't true!"

"What do you mean, not true? Because there are six people instead of one? I made Tityrus be alone to distill the monotony; it's an artistic technique. You don't expect me to have all six of them go fishing, do you?"

"I am quite sure they do different things in real life!"

"And if I described them, they would seem too different. Narrated events never keep the same respective values that they have in life. You have to change them to preserve their truth. What matters is to represent the feeling they give me."

"But what if that feeling is false?"

"A feeling, my dear, is never false. Haven't you ever read that errors arise from making judgments? Anyway, why tell the same thing six times? since the impression they give is the same, exactly the same, all six times ... Do you want me to tell you what they do in real life?"

"Go ahead, tell me," Angela said. "You seem annoyed."

"Not at all!" I cried. "The father writes things, the mother is a housewife, the older son gives lessons, the younger son takes lessons, the older girl limps, the younger girl is too little to do anything. There's the cook too. The wife's name is Ursula ... And you realize that every one of them does the same exact thing every day!!!"

"Maybe that's because they're poor?" Angela said.

"Of course that's why! But now do you understand *Marshlands*?! —Richard, right after he left school, lost his father, a widower. He had to work. There was only a small inheritance, and an older brother took it all. But working these ridiculous jobs, think about it! jobs that don't give you anything except money! in offices, copy at such and such per page! instead of traveling! He's never seen anything, never has anything interesting to say, he reads the newspapers so that he'll have something to talk about—when he has time. Every hour of the day is already spoken for. His destiny is never to do anything else until he dies. —He married a woman with even less money than him, because it was the right thing to do, not for love. Her name is Ursula. —Oh, I've already told you that. —They have turned marriage into a slow apprenticeship in love; by now they have come to love each other very much, and to tell me about it. They love their children very much. Their children love them very much. There's the cook too. —On Sunday evening they all play bingo. I almost forgot the grandmother, she plays too, but since she can't see the cards anymore, they all whisper that she doesn't count. Ah, Angela! Richard! Everything in his life exists to stop up the gaps, fill in the cavernous holes—everything, including his family. He was born a widower. Every day the same pathetic last resorts, the same substitutes for all the better things. After all that, you shouldn't think badly of him—he is extremely virtuous. Plus he thinks he's happy."

"What's this! Are you sobbing?" Angela said.

"Never mind, it's just nerves. —Angela, darling, don't you think that, all things considered, our lives are lacking in any real adventure?"

"What can we do about it?" came her gentle reply. "Do you want to take a little trip, just the two of us? Look—Saturday, are you free?"

"Angela, you don't really mean . . . the day after tomorrow?!"

"Why not? We'll leave bright and early; you're having dinner here the night before, with Hubert. You can sleep here . . . And now good night," Angela said, "I'm going to bed. It's late and you've tired me out. The maid has prepared your room."

"No, darling, I won't stay—I'm sorry, I am far too excited. I have a lot I need to write before I go to bed. See you tomorrow. I'm going home."

I wanted to consult my daily planner. I left almost at a run, especially since it was raining and I had no umbrella. As soon as I got home I wrote, for a day in the following week, this thought, about Richard but not only about Richard:

"The virtue of the meek: acceptance. It fits them so well, some of them, that you seem to understand that their life is made to the measure of their soul. Above all, do not feel sorry for them: their condition is right for them. How awful! They no longer perceive mediocrity, as long as it is not a question of mediocrity of fortune. —What I blurted out to Angela is true nonetheless: things happen to everyone according to their appropriative affinities. Everyone experiences only what is right for them. That means that if someone is happy with his mediocrity, he thereby proves that it suits him, and nothing else will happen. Destinies made to measure. The need to split one's clothes open, the way a plane tree or eucalyptus splits its bark as it grows . . ."

"I'm writing much too much of this," I told myself. "Four words would have been enough. —But I don't like aphorisms. Now what about this astounding proposition of Angela's."

I opened my planner to this Saturday, and on the page for that day I read:

"Try to get up at six. —Vary my emotions.

"Write to Lucien and Charles.

"Find the equivalent of *nigra sed formosa* for Angela.

"Hope to finish Darwin.

"Visit: Laure (explain *Marshlands*), Noémi, Bernard. Devastate Hubert (important).

"Try to cross the Pont de Solférino around dusk.

"Think up epithets for *fungosities*."

That was everything. I picked up my pen, crossed it all out, and instead wrote simply: "Take a little pleasure-trip with Angela." Then I went to bed.

THE BANQUET

THIS MORNING, after a very restless night, I woke up feeling slightly sick; I drank a little herbal tea instead of my bowl of milk, for variety. The day's page in my planner was blank, which meant: *Marshlands.* That is what I do: reserve for work the days when I haven't decided to do anything else. I wrote all morning. I wrote:

TITYRUS'S JOURNAL
I have crossed great moors, vast plains, interminable expanses; even in the low hills, the barely rising earth seeming still to sleep. I love roaming past the peat bogs; paths have been made there, where the packed earth is less spongy, more solid. Everywhere else the ground gives way and the layers of moss sink underfoot; the moss is full of water, soft, with secret drainages somewhere that let it dry out. It also grows on the heather and on a kind of squat pine tree; Lycopodiaceae roots creep there; the water collects into dark stagnant puddles in places. I live in the lowlands, and have little desire to haul myself up the hills, from where, I well know, there is nothing different to be seen. I never look into the distance, even though an overcast sky does have its appeal.

Sometimes, a marvelous iridescence spreads over the surface of the stagnant water—the most beautiful butterflies' wings are nothing compared to it; this mottled membrane is made of decomposing matter. Night wakens phosphorescence on the lakes, and the marshland will-o'-the-wisps rising over those lakes seem the phosphorescence's sublimation.

Marshes! Who, who can tell of your charms? Tityrus!

I mustn't show these pages to Angela, I thought. They make Tityrus seem happy.

I went on to make the following notes:

Tityrus buys an aquarium and puts it in the middle of his greenest room, rejoicing at the thought that the whole landscape outside can be found within it. He puts in it nothing but mud and water; an unknown population lives in the mud, going about their business for his amusement. The water is always murky, only what comes right up to the glass sides can be seen, and in it he likes to watch the alternation of sun and shadow, now more yellow, now more gray—lights that come in through the closed shutters and cross the water —There is always more life in bodies of water than he would have thought . . .

Just then Richard came in; he invited me to have lunch with him on Saturday, and I was delighted to be able to tell him that I would be out of town on that very day. —He seemed stunned, and left without another word.

A little later, after a succinct breakfast, I went out myself. I paid a visit to Étienne, who was correcting the proofs of his play. He told me that I was quite right to write *Marshlands*, because, according to him, I was not put on this earth to write plays. I took my leave. On the street I ran into Roland, who walked me to Abel's, where I found Claudius and Urban, the poets, in the process of asserting that it was impossible to write plays in this day and age. Even though they disagreed with each other's reasons, they were in accord that the theater should be abolished. Moreover, they said that I was quite right to not write poetry anymore, because I was bad at it. In came Theodore, then Walter, whom I can't stand. I left, Roland with me. As soon as we were back outside, I began:

"This life is unbearable! Can you bear it, my friend?"

"Pretty well," he said. "Why is it unbearable?"

"It could be different and yet it isn't—and that is enough to make it unbearable. Our every action is so well known that a stand-in could do it, repeating our words from yesterday to make our phrases of tomorrow. Thursday is Abel's day to receive visitors—he would have been no less astonished not to see Urban, Claudius, Walter, and you come in as we would be not to find him at home! It's not that I'm complaining, but I couldn't stand it a moment longer—I'm leaving— I'm taking a trip."

"You?" Roland said. "Huh! Where, and when?"

"The day after tomorrow. Where? I don't know... But, my friend, you must realize that if I knew where I was going and what I was to do there, then to go there and do it would not free me from my suffering. I am leaving simply to leave; the whole point is surprise—the unexpected—you see?—the unexpected! I am not suggesting you come with me, because I am taking Angela—but why on earth don't you go somewhere too, it doesn't matter where, and leave these hopeless cases to stagnate here?"

"Sorry," Roland said, "I'm not like you. When I go somewhere, I like to know where I'm going."

"So pick somewhere! What can I suggest . . . Africa! Have you been to Biskra? The sunlight on the sand, just think of it! and the palm trees! Roland! Roland! The camels! Think about it: the same miserable sun that we can barely see between the roofs, behind the dust of the city, is shining there too, down in Africa; everything is available everywhere. What are you waiting for? Ah, Roland! It's the airlessness here, not just boredom, that makes us yawn. Will you go?"

"My friend," Roland said, "there may be very pleasant surprises indeed awaiting me down there—but I am too busy to go—so I would rather not want to. I cannot go to Biskra."

"But the whole point is to leave behind the duties that hold you here. —Or do you accept the fate of being tied down forever? It's all the same to me, you understand: I am leaving on a different journey—but remember, we only live once, perhaps, and think how small the circle of your little activities really is!"

"Ah, my friend, don't insist," he said. "I have real reasons why I need to stay, and your argument bores me. I cannot go to Biskra."

"All right, never mind," I said. "Anyway, here's my house—all right then! Goodbye for now, for some time—and would you be so kind as to tell everyone I'm leaving?"

I went inside.

At six o'clock, my great friend Hubert arrived; he had just left a committee meeting for one of his businesses. He said:

"People have been telling me about *Marshlands*!"

"People? Who??" I asked, in a state of great excitement.

"Friends . . . You know, they don't like it very much; someone even said that you would do better to write something else."

"Don't tell me any more."

"You know," he continued, "I don't know about these things; I just listen; as long as you enjoy writing *Marshlands*—"

"But I don't enjoy it at all!" I cried. "I am writing *Marshlands* because . . . Well, let's talk about something else . . . I'm taking a trip."

"Huh!" exclaimed Hubert.

"Yes," I said, "there comes a time when you need to get out of the city for a while. I am leaving the day after tomorrow; I don't know where to . . . And I'm taking Angela."

"What! At your age?"

"But my friend, she's the one who asked me. I'm not suggesting you come with us, because I know you are very busy . . ."

"And you'd rather be alone with each other. That's fine. Will you be gone long?"

"Not too long; there are constraints, of time and money, but the important thing is to get out of Paris. It takes very energetic methods to get out of a city, like express trains; the hard part is getting past the suburbs." I stood up so that I could pace back and forth and get worked up. "All the stations you have to pass through before the true countryside! People get off at every station, like runners falling at the start of a race; the train cars empty out. —Travelers! Where are the travelers? —Those who remain are on business; the stokers and engine-drivers, who go all the way to the end, stay in the engine cab. Besides, at the other end of the line there is nothing but another city. —Countryside! Where is the countryside?"

"My dear friend," Hubert said, pacing as well, "you're exaggerating. The countryside starts where the cities stop, simple as that."

"But my dear friend," I went on, "that's just it: the cities do *not* stop, and then after them come the suburbs...You seem to have forgotten the suburbs—everything that there is between two cities. Smaller houses, set farther apart from each other, even uglier than the city: cityness dragged out; vegetable gardens! Embankments lining the road. The road! Everyone has to keep to the road, and cannot travel anywhere else..."

"You should put that in *Marshlands*," Hubert said.

Now that really made me mad.

"My poor friend, have you really never understood anything about a poem's reason for being? Its nature? Where it comes from? A book...A book is sealed, Hubert, full, as smooth as an egg. You can't put anything else in it, not a pin, except by force, which would shatter its form to pieces."

"So, you have filled your egg?" Hubert said.

"But, my dear friend," I cried, "no one can fill an egg; eggs are born full! Anyway, it's already in *Marshlands*...Plus I think it's asinine to say that I would do better to write something else...asinine! Do you hear me?

"Write something else! First of all, I don't want anything better; try to understand that here too there are embankments on either side, just like elsewhere; our roads are those we cannot but travel, our works those we cannot but write. I take up my position here because no one else has; I choose a subject by elimination, and it is *Marshlands* because I am sure that there will never be anyone so desperate that he comes to work my land; that is what I tried to express with the words: *I am Tityrus, and alone.* —I read you that part, but you didn't pay attention . . . Plus, how many times have I asked you never to talk to me about writing!

"By the way—" I went on, as a way of changing the subject, "—are you coming to Angela's tonight? She's having some people over."

"Some men of letters, you mean. No thanks," he said. "As you know, I don't like those crowded parties where people do nothing but talk; I thought you found them stifling too."

"That's true," I said, "but I don't want to offend Angela; she asked me specially. Besides, I want to see Hamilcar there, to tell him how stifling it is. Angela's living room is much too small for these parties; I will try to tell her so; I will go so far as to use the word *tiny* . . . Plus I have to talk to Martin."

"Up to you," Hubert said. "I must go now; goodbye."

He left.

I arranged my papers; I had dinner and, while chewing, thought about the trip, repeating to myself the words: "Just one day left!" —Toward the end of the meal, I felt so moved by this proposal of Angela's that I felt obliged to write these words to her: "*Perception begins with a change of sensation. Thence the need to travel.*"

Then, having put the letter in an envelope, I calmly made my way to her apartment.

Angela lives on the fifth floor.

On days when she hosts soirées, she puts a bench in front of her door and another on the second landing, in front of Laure's apartment. You can catch your breath; prepare for the lack of air; they are way stations on the ascent. I too, out of breath, sat down on the first bench and, taking a sheet of paper out of my pocket, tried to formulate arguments to present to Martin. I wrote:

Not going out: that is a mistake. In any case, one cannot go out, but that is because one doesn't.

No! That's not it! Start over. I tore up the page.

What I need to express is that everyone, despite being cooped up, thinks he is outside. Oh how wretched my life is! An example.—At that very moment, someone came up the stairs: it was Martin. He said:

"So! Hard at work?"

I answered: "Good evening, my friend. I am just now writing to you. Don't interrupt me. You can wait for me on the bench upstairs."

He went upstairs.

I wrote:

Not going out: that is a mistake. In any case, one cannot go out, but that is because one doesn't. —One doesn't go out because one thinks one is already outside. If we knew we were cooped up, we would at least want to go out.

No! That's not it, that's not it! Start over. I tore up the page.

What I need to express is that everyone thinks he is outside because he doesn't look. And that he doesn't look because he is blind. Oh how wretched my life is! I don't understand it at all . . . Then again, this is a terrible place to do any writing.

I took out another sheet of paper. At that very moment, someone came up the stairs: it was Alexandre, the philosopher. He said:

"So! Hard at work?"

Absorbed in my task, I answered: "Hello. I am writing to Martin; he's on the bench upstairs.—Have a seat, I'm almost done . . . Oh, there's no room?"

"It doesn't matter," Alexandre said, "I have my collapsible cane seat." He unfolded his implement and sat down to wait.

"All right, finished," I said, and, leaning on the banister, I shouted, "Martin! Are you up there?"

"Yes!" he cried. "I am waiting for you. Bring your bench."

So, since I feel almost entirely right at home when I am at Angela's, I lugged the bench up the stairs; there, once all three of us were seated, Martin and I exchanged sheets of paper while Alexandre waited.

On my page, it said:

Staying blind so you think you're happy. Believing you see clearly so as not to have to try to see, since:
The only thing you can see is your own unhappiness.

On his page, it said:

Being happy that you're blind. Believing you see clearly so as not to have to try to see, since:
Seeing yourself can only make you unhappy.

"Martin!" I cried, "it is precisely what you celebrate that I deplore! And I must be right, since I deplore the fact that you celebrate it, while you can't possible celebrate that I deplore it. —Let's start over."

Alexandre waited some more.

"Almost finished," I said to him. "We'll explain it to you later."

We took our pages back.
I wrote:

You remind me of people who translate Numero deus impare gaudet *as* The number two is not a good pair *and don't see anything wrong with that. Now if it were true that unevenness carried with it the promise of happiness—I mean, of freedom—then one would indeed have to say to this number two:* "I am afraid, my poor friend, you are not that: not odd. For that state to content you, you must at least try to attain it."

He wrote:

You remind me of people who translate Et dona ferentes *as* Beware of Greeks *and forget all about the gifts. —Now if it were true that every gift concealed a Greek who takes us prisoner at once, then I would say to this Greek:* "Kind Greek, give and take; then we'll be even. I'm your man, that's true, but if I weren't you would have given me nothing." *For "Greek," read "Necessity," which takes as much as it gives and nothing more.*

We exchanged pages. Some moments passed.

He wrote at the bottom of my page: "*The more I think about it, the more I think your example is idiotic, because ultimately...*"

I wrote at the bottom of his page: "*The more I think about it, the more I think your example is idiotic, because ultimately...*"

Since both of the pages were now full, we each turned over our respective sheet of paper—but something was already written on the back of his:

—The bliss of following rules. Be happy. Come up with a model menu.
1st — Soup (à la Huysmans)
2nd — Steak (à la Barrès)
3rd — Selection of vegetables (à la Gabriel Trarieux)
4th — Demijohn of Evian (à la Mallarmé)
5th — Golden-green Chartreuse (à la Oscar Wilde)

Already written on mine was simply the poetic thought I had had in the botanical garden:

Tityrus smiled.

Martin said, "Who's Tityrus?"
I replied: "I am Tityrus."
"Ah, then you do smile sometimes!"
"Wait a moment, my friend, let me explain ..." (You let yourself go just once, and look what happens!) "Tityrus is me and also not me—Tityrus is the fool; he is me, he is you, he is all of us ... Now don't laugh like that—you're upsetting me—I take 'fool' in the sense of 'infirm'; he does not always keep his wretchedness in mind; that's what I was saying just now. We all have our forgetful moments, but you have to understand that what you have there is nothing but a poetic thought ..."
Alexandre was reading the pages. Alexandre is a philosopher; I never trust what he says, and so never respond to it.
—He smiled and, turning to me, began by saying:

"It seems to me that what you call a 'free act' would be, according to you, an act dependent on nothing; now follow what I'm saying: detachable; note the progression of my argument: eliminable; behold my conclusion: worthless. I say reattach yourself to everything, and do not ask for contingency—in the first place, you will never get it, and secondly, how would it help you if you did?"

I said nothing, as usual. When a philosopher answers you, he makes it impossible for you to understand in the slightest what you had asked him.

We heard people coming upstairs: Clément, Prosper, Kasimir.

"Well," they said, seeing Alexandre sitting with us on the benches, "have you become Stoics? Let's go in, shall we, Gentlemen of the Portico?"

I thought their little joke was pretentious. So much so, in fact, that I felt I must wait for them to go in first before I could.

Angela's living room was already full. She herself was making the rounds among her guests, smiling, offering coffee and brioches. As soon as she saw me, she hurried over:

"Ah, here you are!" she said in a low voice. "I'm a little worried that it's getting boring; do recite some poetry for us."

"But Angela," I said, "it will be just as boring if I do—plus you know I don't know any."

"You do, you do, you've always just written something or other..."

Just then, Hildebrand came over:

"Ah," he said, extending his hand, "how delightful to see

you. I have not yet had the pleasure of reading your latest book, but my friend Hubert tells me it's wonderful ... And it seems that this evening you will favor us with a poetry reading ..."

Angela had already sneaked off.

Up came Ildevert:

"Well," he said, "so," he said, "you are writing *Marshlands*?"

"How did you know that?" I cried.

"What do you mean? It's all anyone's talking about," he said (exaggerating). "It seems as though it will even be different from your last book—which I have not yet had the pleasure of reading, but my friend Hubert has spoken of it to me often. And now you are going to read us some lines, are you not?"

"Not fishing lines, I hope," said Isidore, moronically, "I hear that *Marshlands* is full of them. That's what Hubert says. My dear friend, what is *Marshlands* anyway?"

Valentin came up to us, and now that so many people were listening at once, I got confused.

"*Marshlands*," I began, "is the story of neutral ground, that which belongs to us all ... or better: the terrain of the normal person, the place where we all begin—the story of the third person, about whom one speaks—who lives in us all, who does not die with us. In Virgil, he is called Tityrus. And Virgil explicitly says he is *lying down*—'*Tityre recubans*.' *Marshlands* is the story of Man Lying Down."

"I see!" said Patras. "I thought it was the story of a swamp."

"Sir," I said, "views may differ, the facts remain. But please, try to understand, the only way to say the same thing to everyone—the same thing, you hear me?—is to change its form to suit each new spirit. —At the moment, *Marshlands* is the story of Angela's living room."

"In short, it seems you haven't quite made up your mind yet," remarked Anatole.

Up came Philoxenus.

"Everyone," he said, "is waiting to hear your poetry."

"Shh! Shh!" Angela exclaimed. "He's going to start his reading."

Everyone fell silent.

"But gentlemen!" I cried, in aggravation, "I have nothing worthwhile to read, I assure you! Now if I am not to oblige you to insist, I will have no choice but to read this unfinished little thing I just happen to have with me..."

"Read! Read!" said several voices.

"All right, gentlemen, if you must..."

I took a sheet of paper out of my pocket, and, without striking a pose, I listlessly read:

A WALK

We took a walk upon the moor
Oh God, please hear us! I implore
We roamed and wandered on the moor
And when the night began to fall
A seat was wished for, by us all:
Our feet were very tired and sore.

Not a word. Apparently no one realized the poem was over. They were still waiting.

"That's it," I said.

Then, from amid the silence, came Angela's voice: "Oh! Wonderful!—You should put it in *Marshlands*."

And since everyone else still said nothing: "Don't you think so, gentlemen? That he should put it in *Marshlands*?"

Then there was a kind of commotion for a moment, while

some asked "*Marshlands*? *Marshlands*? What's that?" and others explained what *Marshlands* was—but still rather uncertainly.

I was speechless, but just then Carolus, the erudite physiologist, obsessed as he was with returning to the source, came up to me with a questioning look on his face.

"*Marshlands*?" I began at once. "It is the story of animals who live in dark and gloomy caves, losing their sight from not making use of it. —And now please leave me alone, I feel terribly hot."

However, Evaristus, the subtle critic, argued:

"I'm afraid that, as a subject, you may have hit on something the least little bit too specialized."

"But sir," I had to reply, "there is no such thing as a subject that is too specialized. *Et tibi magna satis*, as Virgil writes—and that, precisely, is my subject, deplore it though I do.

"Art means depicting a specialized subject with such power that the generality on which it depends can be understood in it. It can only be expressed very badly in abstract terms, because the subject is itself already an abstract thought—but surely you will understand what I'm saying if you consider how a whole enormous landscape passes through a keyhole when your eye gets close enough to the door. Someone who sees nothing but a lock would see the whole world through that lock if only he knew that he needed to bend down. It is enough if one creates the possibility of generalization; it is the reader's job, the critic's job, to make the generalization."

"That makes your job much easier, doesn't it," he said.

"Otherwise it would make yours impossible," I replied, nearly suffocated. He moved off. "Ah!" I thought. "Now I can breathe!"

Precisely then, Angela took me by the sleeve: "Come here," she said, "I have to show you something."

And, pulling me over to the curtain, she discreetly raised it to show me a big black blot on the windowpane, making a loud noise.

"I had a fan put in, so now you can't complain that it's too hot," she said.

"My dear Angela!"

"The only thing is that since it makes such a noise, I have had to keep the curtains closed over it."

"Ah! That's what it is! But, darling, it's much too small!"

"They told me at the store that this was the model to use for literary gatherings. The next larger size was for political meetings, but then we wouldn't be able to hear each other."

Just then, Barnaby the moralist came over and tugged at my sleeve, saying: "Various friends of yours have told me enough about *Marshlands* to give me a clear picture of what you're trying to do, and I have come to warn you that to me it seems both useless and unpleasant.

"You want to force people to act, because stagnation horrifies you—but you do not consider that the more you intervene before their act, the less their act results from them. Your responsibility is all the greater; theirs is equally and oppositely diminished. Now, only our own responsibility for our acts makes them matter to us—their appearance means nothing. You cannot teach someone to want: *velle non discitur*. You will simply influence them. And what's the point if you've merely procreated a few worthless actions!"

"So," I told him, "you want us to remain disinterested in others, because you deny that we can do anything with them."

"It's very hard to do anything with them, that much is certain, and for those of us who do, our role is not to engender great acts more or less indirectly, but to make their responsibility for small acts greater and greater."

"To increase the fear of acting at all, you mean? What you will increase is not responsibility, but scruples. And thus you will further limit freedom. The truly responsible act is the free act; our acts are no longer free; what I want is not to create acts but to clear a path for freedom..."

He smiled subtly, to underline the wit of what he was about to say, namely: "So, if I understand what you're saying, you want to force people into freedom."

"When I see sick people around me, it makes me anxious!" I cried. "And if I don't try to cure them—for fear, as you say, of diminishing the value of their cure—at least I try to show them that they're sick. And try to tell them, too."

Galeas walked over, solely to slip in this stupid remark: "You cure a sick man not by showing him his sickness, but by presenting him with the spectacle of health. They should paint a normal person above every hospital bed and line the corridors with copies of the Farnese Hercules."

Then Valentin, who had just turned up, said: "First of all, the normal person is not named Hercules..."

At once everyone said: "Shh! Shh! The great Valentin Knox is speaking!"

He said: "I don't think health is so very desirable. It is merely equilibrium, a mediocrity in all things, the absence of any hypertrophy. The only thing of any value is what makes us different from others; idiosyncracy is our valuable illness. In other words, what matters in us is what we alone possess, what cannot be found in another, what this *normal person* of yours does *not* have—in short, what you call sickness.

"Thus you must cease to regard *sickness* as a lack: on the contrary, it is an excess. A hunchbacked man is a man plus a hunchback. I would argue that you should see health as a lack of sickness.

"We don't care at all about the *normal person*; I would say in fact that we can eliminate him altogether—since after all, we can find another one wherever we want. He is the highest common factor of humanity: that which, in math, given a set of numbers, you can remove from each without taking away its *individual quality*. The *normal person* (how annoying this term is) is the residue, the prime matter that you find at the bottom of the alembic after distillatory heat has subtilized the particularities. He is the pigeon primeval, reconstituted by crossing rare varieties—a gray pigeon, whose colored feathers have all fallen away, leaving nothing to distinguish him."

Seized with enthusiasm because he had started to talk about gray pigeons, I longed to shake his hand. Instead, I exclaimed: "Valentin! Valentin!"

He said simply: "Silence, man of letters! First of all, I only care about the insane, and you are frightfully reasonable."

Then he went on: "The normal person is the man I saw on the street and called by my own name, thinking at first that I had run into myself. I held out my hand to him and cried: 'My poor Knox! How drab you look today! And what have you done with your monocle?' The real surprise was that Roland, with whom I was taking this walk, called the man by *his* name. He said, at the same time as I spoke: 'Poor Roland! What's happened to your beard?' Then, since this individual was boring us, we eliminated him without a pang of remorse. He had nothing new to offer us. He, incidentally, said nothing at all, the pitiful creature. Do you know who this is, this normal person? It is the third person, about whom one speaks..."

He turned to me; I turned to Ildevert and Isidore, and said: "See! What did I tell you?"

Valentin continued in a very loud voice, looking at me: "In Virgil, he is named Tityrus: the one who does not die with us, and lives on in everyone." Then he added, bursting out laughing (at me): "That is why it doesn't matter much if he's killed."

And Ildevert and Isidore, guffawing with laughter as well, cried: "So get rid of Tityrus!!!"

Infuriated, unable to restrain myself any longer, I too exclaimed: "Shh! Shh! I'm going to say something!" And I began to speak, it didn't matter what I was saying.

"Yes, gentlemen, yes! Tityrus is sick!!! We are all sick, every last one of us and all our lives long, not only during the times of madness when we fall prey to obsessive doubts: Did we lock the door? let's go check it. Did we put on our tie this morning? let's feel to make sure. Did we button our fly tonight? double-check. Look! Madruce there wasn't quite sure! Nor was Borace! You see what I mean.

"Notice that we know perfectly well that we've done whatever it is—doing it again is a kind of sickness, the sickness of retrospection. We do it again precisely because we *have* done it; every one of our acts from yesterday seems to want us again today, like a child to whom we have given life and who demands from then on that we keep it alive..."

I was exhausted, and I could tell I was speaking poorly.

"We feel that we have to continue everything we start— hence our fear of committing too many acts, we are afraid we will then be dependent on too much—for every act, once we do it, instead of becoming a starting point for us, becomes the cavernous bed into which we fall back—*recubans*."

"What you're saying," Ponce began, "is very strange..."

"No it's not, not at all—and there is no way I should put it into *Marshlands*!...I was saying that our individuality can no longer be detached from the way we act—it lies in the act itself—in the two acts we perform (a trill)—in the three acts. Who is Bernard? He is who you meet at Octave's on Thursdays. Who is Octave? He is who Bernard goes to see on Thursdays. Is that it? He is also the one who goes to see Bernard on Mondays. —Who is...who are we all, gentlemen? We are those who go to Angela's on Friday nights."

"But," Lucien said, to be polite, "first of all, so much the better; secondly, you may be sure that this is our only point of contact!"

"Sacre bleu! I know full well that when Hubert comes to see me every day at six o'clock, he can't very well be visiting you at the same time, but what's the difference if the person who comes to see you every day is Bridget? —What does it even matter if Joachim sees her only every third day? —Am I a statistician? —No! but I'd rather walk on my hands *today* than walk on my feet...*the same as yesterday!*"

"Still, it seems to me that that's actually what you're doing," Tullius said, moronically.

"That's exactly what I'm complaining about! I did say 'I'd rather,' did I not? Besides, if I tried to do it nowadays, on the street, they'd lock me up as a madman. And that's precisely what I can't stand: that everything outside of us —the law, morality, sidewalks—seems to determine our relapses and lay claim to our monotony, while underneath it all, everything conforms so perfectly to our love of repetition."

"So what are you complaining about?" Tancredo and Gaspard burst out.

"The fact that no one is complaining! Resigning oneself

to something bad only aggravates it—it becomes a vice, gentlemen, because one ends up liking it. What I am complaining about, sir, is that no one rebels: that we eat our mush and act like we're dining magnificently, and look smug after a ninety-nine-cent meal. The fact that no one fights back against..."

"Oh-ho! Oh-ho!" came the cries from several quarters. "Now you're calling for the revolution?!"

"Not at all, gentlemen, not at all! I am no revolutionary. You won't let me finish. I'm saying that we don't fight... on the inside. I'm not talking about the distribution of wealth, I'm talking about us: our morality..."

The room erupted in chaos. "You criticize people for living the way they do, —then you deny that they can live any differently, —and you reproach them for being happy to live that way —but if they like it, then... then... but... really, what-in-the-world-do-you-want???"

I was covered in sweat and completely bewildered; I answered desperately: "What, what do I want? What I want, gentlemen—me, personally—is to finish *Marshlands*."

At this, Nicodemus dashed up out of the crowd to shake my hand and cry: "Ah! What a great day it will be when you do!" This made all the others turn their backs.

"What do you mean?" I said. "Have you read *Marshlands*?"

"No," he replied, "but my friend Hubert has told me a lot about it."

"Ah! He told you—"

"Yes, the story of the fisherman who decides that bloodworms are so good that he eats them instead of baiting his lines—so he doesn't catch anything. Obviously. That's so funny!"

He had not understood a thing. —I have to start over

again, from the beginning. But I am so worn out! And I have to say that that is the very thing I want to make them understand: that one has to start over to make them understand—always—it is so confusing; I can't go on, oh! I've already said that...

And since when I am at Angela's I feel almost entirely right at home, I went over to her, took out my pocket watch, and cried as loud as I could:

"My word, darling, look how terribly late it is!"

Then everyone took their own watch out of their own pocket at the same time and cried: "My goodness it's late!"

Only Lucien insinuated, to be polite, "Last Friday it was even later!"—But no one paid any attention to his comment (I simply told him: "Your watch is slow"). Everyone ran off to find their coats; Angela shook her guests' hands, still smiling, and offered them the last of the brioches. Then she leaned over the banisters to see everyone down. —I waited for her on an ottoman, shattered.

When she returned, I began by saying: "What a total nightmare this party was! Oh, these writers, these writers, Angela!!! Every last one of them unbearable!!!"

"But that's not what you were saying the other day," she replied.

"That's because I hadn't seen them here at your apartment, Angela. —And another thing, it's dreadful how many of them there were! You simply can't have so many over at once, darling!"

"But I didn't invite them all," she said. "The problem was that each of them brought several others."

"You looked so dazed in the middle of them all...You should have asked Laure to come upstairs; you would have given each other strength to keep up a good face."

"But it's because I saw you so worked up," she said. "I thought you were about to start chewing the chairs."

"Angela, darling, it's because otherwise everyone would have been so bored . . . And it was so stifling hot in your living room! Next time no one can come in without a ticket. —And what, may I ask, did you mean with this little fan of yours? First of all, nothing upsets me more than an object turning round and round in the same place; you should know that by now! Secondly, what a horrible noise it makes as it turns! You could hear it behind the curtain the moment you stopped talking. Everyone was wondering: 'What's that?' And you realize I couldn't exactly tell them: 'It's Angela's fan!' There, you can hear it now, grinding away. It's unbearable, darling! Turn it off, I beg of you!"

"But you can't turn it off," Angela said.

"Aghh! It too!" I cried. "Well, let's talk louder, darling! —What's this? You're crying?"

"Not at all," she said, her face quite red.

"Too bad!" And, gripped with lyricism, I bellowed to drown out the sound coming from the noisemaker: "Angela! Angela! The time has come! Let us depart these intolerable environs! Shall we not suddenly hear the grand sea air sweeping across the beaches, my darling? —I know that when one is with you one has only little thoughts, but perhaps this wind will raise them higher . . . Goodbye for now! I need to take a walk. It's only tomorrow, just think! then we're leaving on our trip.

"Do think of it, darling Angela, think of it!"

"All right then, bye," she said. "Go sleep at home."

I left her. I practically ran home, got undressed, got into bed, but not to sleep, I am always agitated after watching other people drink coffee. Besides, I felt no little distress, and I asked myself: "Did I really do everything I could to convince them? I should have found stronger arguments for Martin . . . And Gustave! —Oh, so Valentin only likes madmen—and he called me 'reasonable'! How could he! I haven't done a single thing today that wasn't absurd. Though I realize that that isn't exactly the same thing . . . And now, thought of mine, why do you stop me and fix me with your gaze like that of a wild-eyed owl? —'Revolutionary,' huh, maybe that's what I am after all, by dint of sheer horror at its opposite. Oh, how horrible it makes you feel when you've tried to stop feeling horrible! —Not to be able to make oneself under-stood . . . Still, it's true, what I told them—since I suffer from it. —Do I suffer from it? —My word! Sometimes I no longer understand a thing, neither what I want nor whom I want to slap in the face. I feel like I'm fighting my own shadow, and that . . . My God, my God! that's a truly oppressive thought, and others' thoughts are an even deader weight than matter. It's as though every idea, as soon as you touch it, avenges itself upon you; these ideas are like the ghouls that walk by night and rest on your shoulders, feed upon you, weigh all the more heavily upon you the weaker they have made you . . . Now that I have started to look for equivalents for these thoughts, so as to make them clearer to others—I can't stop; retrospections; (these metaphors are ridiculous;) I feel myself succumbing little by little to all the sicknesses I am describ-ing, and reproaching others for; I keep for myself all the suffering I cannot manage to make them feel. —Now it seems to me that the sensation I have of it only makes my sickness worse, and that when all is said and done, maybe other people are not sick after all. —In which case they are right not to suffer, and I have no right to reproach them.

And yet I live like they do, and living that way is what makes me suffer... Ah! My head, it is in despair! I want people to worry—I try so hard to make them, and I only feel anxious myself... Wait a minute, a phrase! Let me make a note of it." I took a sheet of paper out from under my pillow, relit my candle, and wrote down these simple words:

To be seized by one's worries.

I blew out my candle.

"... My God, my God! before I go to sleep there is one more small thing I want to examine here. You take a small idea—you could just as well have left it alone... —What!... Huh?... Nothing, it's me talking. —I was just saying that you could have just as well left it alone... What!... Huh?... Ah, I was just dropping off to sleep... —no, I wanted to think some more about this small idea that gets bigger; I don't entirely grasp the progression; now it's huge, the idea —and it's taken hold of me —to live off of me, yes, I am its means of existence; it's heavy—I have to present it, represent it to the world.—It has taken hold of me so that I'll haul it around to everyone.—It weighs upon me as heavily as God Himself... Damnation! another phrase!" I took out another sheet of paper; I lit my candle; I wrote:

It must increase, but I must decrease.

"That's in the Gospel According to John... Ah! while I'm thinking of it:"—and I took out a third sheet of paper...

. . . .

"I can't remember what I wanted to say...oh, never mind! I have a headache...No, I will lose the thought, lose it... and I would feel a pain in its place, like with a wooden leg... wooden leg...It's not there anymore, but you can still feel it, the thought...the thought...—When you repeat words, it's because you're about to fall asleep; I'll say it again: wooden leg—wooden leg...leg...Oh! I didn't blow out my candle... Yes I did. —Did I blow out my candle?...Yes, since I'm asleep. —And yet when Hubert came back, it wasn't out... but Angela insisted it was...that was when I told her about the wooden leg; because it was stuck in the peat bog; I pointed out to her that I would never be able to run fast enough; the ground here is terribly springy, I said!...like being frog-marshed—no, that's not right...Hey, where's Angela? I start to run a little faster.—Horrors! You just sink right in, it's terrible...I'll never run fast enough...Where is the boat? Have I reached it?...I'm going to jump—oof! whoops!— Welp!...

"Well, if you want, Angela, we'll take a little pleasure-trip in this rowboat. I was just pointing out, my dear, that there is nothing here but sedge grass and lycopodium—lesser potamogetons—and I don't have anything in my pockets— just tiny bits of bread for the fishes...Wait! Where's Angela?... Angela, my love, why did you dissolve in tears tonight?...— and now you're dissolving completely, my dear! —Angela! Angela! Can you hear me? —Look, can you hear? Angela!... and will there be nothing left of you besides this branch of botanical water lilies, nymphaea (I use the word in a sense that is very difficult to appreciate nowadays) that I am about to gather in the river...It's so velvety—absolutely, a carpet!— a springy rug!...So why stay sitting on it, with these two chair legs in your hands? We really have to try to get out from under the furniture! —Monseigneur is coming... especially since it's so suffocating in here, you can't breathe!... Look, here is Hubert's portrait. In the flower of youth... Let's open the door, it's too hot. This other room seems to me a little closer to what I was expecting—only the portrait of Hubert here is not as good; I like the other one better; he looks like a fan—my word! the spitting image of a fan! Why is he giggling?... Let's get out of here. Come, my love... wait! where's Angela? —I was holding her hand so tightly just now; she must have popped down the hall to pack her suitcase. She might have left the timetable... But don't run so fast, I won't be able to keep up with you. —Ah! Wretched existence! another closed door... Luckily they are very easy to open; and I slam them behind me so that Monseigneur can't catch me. —I do believe he's put every one of Angela's guests on my tracks... So many! So many! Men of letters!... Bam! another closed door. —Bam! —Won't we ever get out of this hallway! —Bam! —One after another! I don't know whether I'm coming or going anymore... But I'm running fast now!... Have mercy! there are no more doors at all now. The portrait of Hubert is hanging crooked; it's going to fall; he looks like a fan... a temperature giggulator... This room is much too cramped—I will even employ the word *tiny*. We'll never be able to fit everyone in. They're still coming... I can't breathe! —Aha! through the window! —I'll just shut it behind me; I'll just flutter wretchedly out onto the balcony overlooking the street. —Wait! It's a hallway! Ah! Here they are: —My God, my God, I am going mad... I can't breathe!"

I woke up soaked in sweat; the sheets were tucked in too tight, strapping me down like ropes, so tight that I felt them as a horrible weight on my chest. I made a tremendous effort and raised them up, then threw them off all at once. The air in the room surrounded me; methodically, I breathed. — Coolness—early morning—pale windowpanes . . . Have to make a note of all that; aquarium, —it merges with the rest of the room . . . Just then I shivered; I'm going to catch a cold, I thought; I am definitely catching a cold. —And I stood up, teeth chattering, to pick the covers up off the floor, put them back on the bed, and calmly tuck myself back in to go to sleep.

HUBERT, OR THE DUCK HUNT

Friday

As soon as I woke up, I saw in my daily planner: *Try to get up at six.* It was eight. I picked up my pen; I crossed out the words; I wrote instead: *Get up at eleven.* —Then I went back to bed without reading the rest.

After my horrible night I did not feel well. I had a little herbal tea, instead of milk, for variety's sake; I even had it in bed, my servant having brought it to me there. My daily planner vexed me, and it was on a truly loose sheet of paper that I wrote: "Buy a demijohn of Evian tonight." Then I pinned the sheet to the wall.

"I will stay home to enjoy this water, I will not have dinner with Angela, Hubert will be there anyway. I wouldn't want to bother them. But I'll drop by right after dinner, in the evening, to see if I should have bothered them."

I picked up my pen and wrote:

"Darling, I have a splitting headache. I won't be able to come for dinner; besides, Hubert will be there, and I don't want to bother you. But I'll drop by right after dinner, in the evening. I had a very strange nightmare last night, I'll tell you about it."

I put the letter in an envelope, took another sheet of paper, and very calmly wrote:

Tityrus walked along the edge of the ponds, gathering medicinal plants. He found borage, some quite effective marsh mallow, extremely bitter cornflower. He returned with a spray of simples. Due to the special properties of the plants he had gathered, he went looking for people to treat. There was no one by the ponds. What a shame, he thought. —So he walked toward the salt marshes, where there were fevers, and workers. He went over to them, talked to them, exhorted them, proved to them that they were sick —but one of them said that he wasn't sick; another, to whom Tityrus gave a medicinal flower, planted it in a vase and went to watch it grow; a third one, finally, knew full well that he had a fever, but believed it was good for his health.

So, seeing as in the end no one wanted to get better, and that the flowers were wilting, Tityrus caught the fever himself, so that he would have at least one patient to treat...

At ten o'clock, the doorbell rang: it was Alcides. He said: "Still in bed! Are you sick?"

I said: "No. Hello, my friend. —But I cannot get up before eleven. It's a resolution I've made. What did you want?"

"To say goodbye; I've heard that you're leaving on a trip. Will you be gone long?"

"Not very, very long...With the means I have at my disposal, you understand... But the important thing is to leave. —What? No, I didn't say that so you would go away; but I do have a lot to write, before I...Well, it was very nice of you to come. Goodbye." He left.

I took out a fresh sheet of paper and wrote:

Tityre semper recubans

then went back to sleep until noon.

It's a curious thing, which should be noted down: how an important resolution, the decision to make a great change in one's life, makes all the little daily duties and tasks seem so futile, and thus gives one the strength to send them all to the devil.

This was what gave me the courage to be ruder to Alcides, whose visit so disturbed me, than I would normally have dared to be. —Likewise, having glanced at my planner despite myself and seen the memorandum: "Ten o'clock. Go explain to Magloire why I think he's such a jerk," I had the strength to be happy that I had not gone to see him.

"This planner isn't all bad," I thought, "because if I hadn't written down for this morning what I was supposed to have done, I might have forgotten it, and then I would not have been able to be pleased at not having done it. Herein lies the perpetual delight I take in what I have so felicitously called the *negative unforeseen*: I love it so because it requires so little effort on my part, and thus works for me on normal days."

So, that night, after dinner, I betook myself to Angela's. She was seated at the piano, helping Hubert sing the great duet in *Lohengrin*, which I was delighted to interrupt.

"Angela, my dear," I said as I walked in, "I have not brought a suitcase; and yet I will spend the night here, as you have graciously invited me to, awaiting together with you, no?, our hour of bright and early departure. —A while ago I had to leave various things here that you no doubt have put in my room: country boots, sweater, belt, waterproof riding cap . . . I'll find everything I need. I will not go back home. —This last night before our trip, we must do our very best, think on tomorrow's departure, do nothing that does not prepare for it; we must motivate it, bring it about, make it desirable in every way. Hubert, enchant us with the tale of some past adventure."

"I don't really have time," Hubert said. "It's already late and I have to drop by my insurance company to take care of some documents before the office closes. —Plus, I don't know how to tell stories, and the only ones I have are memories of my hunting expeditions. The one that comes mind is from my great voyage in Judea . . . but it's a terrible story, Angela, I don't know if—"

"Oh! Tell it, please!"

"If you want. Here's the story:

"I was traveling with Bolbos—neither of you know him; he was a great friend from my childhood. Don't bother, Angela, he's dead now. His demise is my story.

"Like me, he was a great hunter. He hunted tigers in the jungle. He was vain as well, and he had had a fur coat made for himself from the skin of a tiger he had personally killed, it was in very poor taste, and he wore it even on hot days, always wide open. He was wearing it on this last night . . . when it made more sense to do so than usual, since it was almost too dark to see and the biting cold was getting colder.

"As you know, the nights are cold in these climes, and it is at night that one hunts the panther. You do it from a swing—it's really quite fun. In the mountains of Edom, there are the well-known stony ravines which the beasts pass through at a given time; nothing is more regular in its habits than a panther, you know, and that is how it is possible to hunt them. —The panther has to be killed from above, for anatomical reasons. Hence the use of the swing, though its advantages only truly become apparent if one shoots and misses. The recoil of the blast actually propels the swing strongly enough to set it in motion: you use very light swings on a panther hunt, they fly up at once, backward, forward, and the frustrated panther springs but cannot catch the hunter—as it certainly would have if he had remained motionless. —'Would have,' did I say? It did! It did, Angela!

"These swings are suspended from either side of the ravine. We each had our own swing; it was late; we were waiting. The panther was due to pass beneath us between midnight and one. I was still young, something of a coward, and yet reckless —or let me say hasty. Bolbos was older and wiser. And as a most excellent friend, familiar with hunting this way, he had let me sit on the better end, so that I would be first to sight the prey."

"Your poetry is worthless," I told him. "Do try to stick to prose."

He went on without having understood what I meant: "At midnight, I loaded my rifle. At a quarter past midnight, the full moon rose above the rocks."

"That must have been beautiful!" Angela said.

"Before long, we could hear the soft, unmistakable whisper that wild beasts make as they stride. It was not far off. At half past midnight, I saw a long, slinking shape coming closer—the panther! Still I waited, until it was right under me. I fired . . .

"Angela, my dear, what can I say? I felt myself suddenly pushed backward on the swing—I felt like I was flying. I was out of reach at once—I had lost my head, but not so much that I . . . Bolbos hadn't fired! What was he waiting for? That was what I couldn't understand. But what I did realize that it is unwise to hunt panthers in pairs: suppose, my dear Angela, that one of you fires even a split second after the other—the angered panther sees the motionless shape—it has time to leap—and the hunter it catches is the one who hadn't fired.

"When I think back on it now, I believe Bolbos wanted to fire but his gun wouldn't go off. These failures happen, even with the best rifles. —When, at the end of my backward arc, beginning to swing forward once more, I saw Bolbos with the panther on top of him, both of them on the swing, lurching back and forth so fast... Really, nothing is more agile than a panther.

"I had to... Think about it, Angela, my dear! —There was nothing I could do but to look on at the scene—swinging back and forth, still swinging; —he swinging now too, beneath the panther—there was nothing I could do! —Use my rifle? Impossible: how could I aim? —I would have liked to at least leave, since the motion was making my heart feel terribly queasy..."

"How stirring that must have been!" Angela said.

"And now goodbye, my dear friends—I must leave you. I am pressed for time. Have a good trip; have fun; don't get home too late. —I'll come see you again on Sunday."

Hubert left.

A vast silence ensued. If I had spoken, I would have said: "Hubert told that story very badly. I didn't know he had traveled to the Holy Land. Is this story true? —You were looking at him with a seemingly rather immoderate admiration as he told it." —But I said nothing; I looked at the fireplace, the flame in the lamp, Angela beside me, both of us beside the fire—the table—the exquisite penumbra of the room—everything that we were going to have to leave behind... Tea was brought in. It was after eleven; we both seemed to be dozing off.

When midnight had ceased to toll, I began:

"I, too, have been hunting."

The astonishment seemed to wake her up in a flash. She said: "You?! You have!? What kind of hunting?"

"A duck hunt, Angela. It was even with Hubert. Long, long ago... But Angela, my dear, why wouldn't I? It's not hunting I have a problem with, it's the guns; I hate the loud bangs. You are mistaken in your judgment of me, I assure you. I have a very active temperament; it's the equipment that gets on my nerves... But Hubert, who is always up to date on the latest inventions, had managed to get for me, through Amédée, a compressed-air rifle to use for the winter."

"Oh! Tell me everything!" Angela said.

"This was not," I went on, "one of those extraordinary rifles that you see only in the big sales, you realize. Besides, I had only rented it. They're terribly expensive, plus I don't like to keep firearms in the house. —A small reservoir of air operates the trigger, through a rubber tube that you run under your armpit; you hold a squeeze bulb in your hand— this one was rather worn-out, it was an old device—and the least pressure on the rubber bulb fires the bullet... I can't explain it any better than that, it's impossible, given your total ignorance in technical matters."

"You should have showed it to me," Angela said.

"Darling, the equipment can only be handled with extraordinary adroitness,—and I've already told you I didn't keep it. Moreover, this one night of hunting, fruitful as it was, was enough to wear out the squeeze bulb once and for all—as I am about to tell you.

"It was a foggy December night. Hubert said to me: 'Are you coming?' and I answered him: 'I am ready.' He took down his hunting gun, and I my rifle; he picked up his birdcalls and boots; we picked up our nickel skates. Then, with the sixth sense particular to hunters, we advanced through the shadows. Hubert knew the path leading to the hut, beside a lake that was well stocked with game, where a peat fire had been simmering for us under its ashes since nightfall. In any case, as soon as we left the park cluttered with its dark pines, the night seemed almost bright. An almost fully inflated moon shone dimly through the ethereal fog, visible not the way it sometimes is—now visible, now not; hidden and then streaming above the clouds. The night was not restless—it was also not peaceful—it was mute, idle, humid, and, would you understand me if I put it this way: *involuntary*. The sky was entirely uniform. You could have turned it over and not found anything different. —If I insist on this point, my tranquil friend, it is to make you truly understand the extent to which this night was an ordinary night.

"Experienced hunters know that this is the best kind of night for waiting in duck blinds.

"We reached the canal, whose icy surface we could make out through the withered reeds due to its brightly polished surface. We put on our skates and glided off without a word. The closer we got to the lake, the more the muddy water, increasingly shallow, was filled with moss and earth and half-melted snow, making our path difficult. The canal gradually vanished. Before long, our skates were a hindrance. We walked.

"Hubert stepped into the hut to get warm; I couldn't stay in there myself because of the thick smoke...

"What I'm about to tell you, Angela, is a dreadful thing! Because, listen: —As soon as Hubert was warm enough, he came out and stepped into the sludgy water; yes, I know he had his boots on, and his waterproof clothes, but, my dear, he did not sink in up to his knees—not up to his waist—he went under entirely! —Don't shudder too much, he did it on purpose! He wanted to disappear completely, to better hide from the ducks. It was a wretched trick, you're about to say... Yes, wasn't it though? I think so too. But as a result the fowl were especially abundant.

"We took up our positions; I, at the bottom of a moored rowboat, waited for the flock to fly overhead. Hubert, once he was well hidden, started to call the ducks, using two bird whistles: one for the call, and one for the reply. The migrating fowl heard the call from a distance; it heard the response; a duck is such a stupid creature that it thought it was hearing its own voice, so they hurried over to be in time to have uttered it, Angela, imagine.

"Hubert's mimicry was perfect. The sky above us grew dark with their triangular cloud; then the noise of their wings grew louder, as they came in for a landing. When they were close enough, I began to fire.

"They were soon so numerous that, to tell you the truth, I hardly bothered to aim: I merely pressed the squeeze bulb a little harder each time. The trigger worked so easily. The only noise it made was the sound a roman candle makes in the air at the moment it bursts—or, rather, the sound of 'Palm!' in a line of Mallarmé's. More often than not I did not hear even that, and if I didn't hold my ear next to the gun barrel I could only tell the bullet had been shot by the sight of another bird falling from the sky. The ducks stayed there for a long time, not hearing any sound. They turned toward the dark water smothered in a grimy crust, and fell, contorted, tearing off leaves with wings they could not close. They tried, before they died, to reach the shelter of the bushes, since the reeds did not conceal them. Feathers lingered, floating on the water, floating in the air, and seemed as light as the wisps of mist... I wondered: When will it end?

"Finally, at daybreak, the last survivors flew off; all at once there was a great sound of wings, which the last dying fowl understood. Then at last Hubert reappeared, covered with leaves and sludge. We unmoored the flat-bottomed rowboat, poled it through the bent stalks, in the dreadful clear light of dawn, and gathered up our victuals. —I had killed more than forty ducks; they all smelled swampy... Wait! What? Have you fallen asleep, my dear Angela?"

The lamp growing dim without oil, the fire sadly dying, the windowpane bathed in the light of dawn: a shred of hope seeming to descend at last, with a shiver, from the storehouses of heaven... Ah! come to us at last, oh drop of celestial dew, and, in this cramped room where we have slept so long, let a dawn appear at last, through the window, in the rain, and let it bring us, through the accumulated shadows, a glint of natural whiteness...

Angela, half-asleep, not hearing what I was saying, quietly woke and murmured: "You should put that..."

"Ach! For pity's sake, don't finish, darling—and especially do not tell me I should put it in *Marshlands*. —First of all, it's already in there. Secondly, you weren't even listening. But I'm not angry—no, I beg you, do not think I am mad at you. Besides I am trying to be happy today. Another day is born, Angela! Look! The gray roofs of the city, the pale light over the suburbs... Will it be... Ah! from what dreary grayness, what sleepless night turned to dust, bitter ash, ah, thought!—will it be your artless kindness, gliding forth undreamt of, dawn, that will deliver us? —The pane in which the morning streams...no...the morning where the window pales...Angela—would wash...would wash...

Lo, we are leaving! I can feel the intoxication of the birds!

"Angela! This is a line of Mallarmé's! I'm misquoting it—it's actually 'I,' not 'we,' but after all, you are leaving with me —Ah! darling, I am taking you with me! —Suitcases! —Let's hurry; I want a jam-packed haversack! Then again, we mustn't bring too much stuff: 'Everything one can't fit into a suitcase is unbearable!' —Barrès said that —Barrès, you know, the politician, my dear! —Oh! It's stifling in here. I can't breathe, let us open the window, if you don't mind! I am in a tizzy. To the kitchen, quick! You never know where you'll eat on a trip. Let us bring four stuffed rolls, some eggs, some sausage, and the veal tenderloin left over from supper last night."

Angela withdrew; I was alone for a moment.

Now, what should I say about that moment? Why not talk about it at least as much as about the following moment—do we know, after all, which things are the important ones? What arrogance there is in *choice*! Let us regard everything with the same insistence. Before the frenzied departure, may I have one more calm meditation. Let us look! Let us look! What do I see?

- Three vegetable sellers walking past.
- A bus, already.
- A doorman sweeping in front of his door.
- Shopkeepers tidying up their shop windows.
- The cook, leaving for the market.
- Schoolboys on their way to school.

- Newspaper kiosks taking deliveries; gentlemen crowding round to buy the day's papers.
- Someone putting out the tables in front of a café…

My God! Please, God, let Angela not come into the room now, I am weeping again…It's nerves, I think; they come over me every time I make a list. —And I'm shivering now too! —Ah, for the love of me, can't we close that window? I'm frozen stiff from this morning air. —Life…the life of others!…is that life?…behold, life! That, after all, is life!!… And what could you say about it to someone else? Exclamations. —Now I'm sneezing. As soon as a thought stops and contemplation begins, I catch cold.

But hark, I hear Angela—Let us hurry!

ANGELA, OR THE LITTLE TRIP

I MUST write down nothing but poetic moments during this trip, because they are more like what I wanted.

In the car that took us to the station, I recited:

> Goats beside the mountain streams;
> Bridges thrown across ravines;
> Rows of larches...
> Ascending with us, I imagine,
> The splendid odor of the resin
> Of pines and larches.

"Oh!" Angela said, "what beautiful poetry!"

"You think so, my dear?" I told her. "No, no, really. I don't say it's terribly bad ... But I don't ultimately think it's very good. I was just improvising. Then again, maybe you're right —maybe it is good after all. The author himself never knows..."

We arrived at the station much too early. In the waiting room we had, indeed, a wait, and a long one too. It was there, sitting next to Angela, that I felt I had to say something nice to her.

"Dear friend, —my dear friend—" I began. "There is in

your smile a sweetness I cannot fully grasp. Might it be because you are so sensitive?"

"I don't know," she replied.

"Sweet Angela! I have never appreciated you as much as I do today."

I also told her: "My charming friend, how delicate the leaps in your trains of thought!" As well as something else I can't remember.

Aristolochia-lined path

Around three o'clock, apropos of nothing, a light shower of rain began to fall.

"It'll pass in a moment," Angela said.

"Why, my darling," I asked her, "why would you bring along only a parasol in such uncertain weather?"

"It's both, it's an en-tout-cas," she told me.

Still, since it was raining harder, and since I am quite afraid of humidity, we retreated to take shelter under the roof of the cider mill we had just left.

From the tops of the pine trees we could see a brown line of processionary caterpillars slowly making their way down, one by one—and at the bottom of the tree, fat patient ground beetles devouring them.

"I didn't see any ground beetles!" Angela said (after I showed her this sentence).

"Me neither, my dear Angela. No caterpillars, either. — Moreover, it's the wrong time of year. But the sentence is true, is it not? It captures the feeling of our trip superbly.

"In the end, it's a good thing that this little trip was such a failure—it's more instructive for you that way."

"Oh! Why do you say that?" Angela replied.

"But, darling, you must understand that the pleasure a trip may bring is purely secondary. One travels to learn something…What? Are you crying, darling?"

"Not at all!" she exclaimed.

"Fine! Too bad. —Still, you are a bit flushed."

SUNDAY

In the daily planner:

Ten o'clock: church.

Go see Richard.

Around five, go with Hubert to visit the impoverished Rosselange family and Grabu, the little gardener.

Remark to Angela how serious I am when I'm joking.

Finish *Marshlands*. —Solemnity.

It was nine o'clock. I felt the gravity of this day in the recrudescence of my agony. I gently rested my head in my hand, and wrote:

"All my life I will have reached out toward an ever so slightly greater light. I have seen all around me, ah!, crowds of people languishing in too-cramped rooms; the sunlight never enters them, the large faded surfaces merely give off a reflection of it around noon, the hour when, on the little streets, you couldn't breathe in the stifling heat. Rays of light, finding no room to disperse, concentrated an unhealthy swoon between the walls of the buildings. Those who saw such things thought of open spaces, rays of sunlight on the foam of the waves and on fields of grain in the prairies . . ."

Angela came in.

I cried: "Angela, darling! It's you!"

She said: "Hard at work? You are sad this morning. I could sense it. I have come."

"Angela, darling! But... Sit down. —Why would I be any sadder this morning?"

"Oh! So you *are* sad? —And it wasn't true, what you said yesterday? You can't really be happy that our trip wasn't everything we'd hoped for."

"Sweet Angela!... I am truly touched by your words. Yes, it's true, I am sad, my darling. This morning my soul is quite desolate."

"I have come to console it," she said.

"Oh, how we relapse, my dear! Everything is so much sadder at the moment. —I had put much hope in our trip, I admit it. I thought it would give my talents a new direction. It was you who suggested the trip to me, that is true, but I had been thinking of it myself, for many years. I feel more clearly now everything I wanted to leave behind, in seeing it upon my return."

"Maybe we didn't go far enough," Angela said. "But it would have taken us two days to go to the seaside, and we did want to be back on Sunday in time for church."

"We had not given nearly enough thought to that coincidence, Angela. And the question remains: How far should we have had to go? How we relapse, my dear Angela! Thinking back on it now: How sad our trip was! —The word 'aristolochia' expresses something of that sadness. —You will remember for a long time that little meal in the damp cider mill, and how, afterward, not saying a word, we shivered.

"Stay—stay with me all morning here, I beg you! I can tell that I am about to burst into tears. It seems to me that I carry *Marshlands* with me always. —*Marshlands* will never bore anyone as much as it has bored me..."

"What if you abandoned it," she said.

"Angela! Angela! You don't understand a thing! I abandon it here; I find it again there. I find it again everywhere. I see other people and I am obsessed with it; this little trip of ours has not freed me from it.

"We do not use up our melancholy, use up our sickness, by remaking our yesterdays on each new day; we use up nothing but ourselves, losing strength every day. —These continuations of the past! I am afraid of dying, my dear Angela. Can we never put anything outside of time—and not be forced to remake it again?

"A work, in the end, that doesn't need us in order to last. But nothing we do lasts a moment beyond when we stop sustaining it. And yet all our acts horrifically endure, they weigh upon us. What weighs on us is the necessity of repeating them. There is something about that I don't entirely understand. —Sorry, just a second..."

Taking out a sheet of paper, I wrote: "*We must sustain our actions even after they cease to be sincere.*"

I went on: "Don't you see, my dear Angela, that is what made our trip a failure... There is nothing we can leave behind, saying: 'THAT EXISTS.' And so we return, to see if everything is still there. —Ah, how wretched our life is! In the end, we never make anyone else do anything! except tow along these drifting wrecks...

"And our relationship, Angela darling! Could anything be so transitory? That, you see, is just what has allowed us to continue it for so long."

"Oh! That's not fair," she said.

"No, my dear —no, it's not that, —but I am trying to make you see what a feeling of sterility it leaves one with."

Then Angela bowed her head and, smiling a little, said,

for convenience's sake: "I can stay tonight. Do you want me to?"

"Oh!" I cried. "What do you mean, darling! If I can't even talk to you about these things anymore without you immediately... —Besides, you must admit you don't really want to; plus you are so delicate, I assure you, and it was while I was thinking of you that I wrote, you remember, the sentence: '*She feared pleasure as something too strong, which might even perhaps kill her.*' You kept insisting that I was exaggerating... No, darling, —no —it may be embarrassing, but —I've even written a few lines on the subject:

> We are not,
> My dear, among those
> Who engender the sons of man.

"(The rest of the piece is very moving, but far too long for me to quote now.) —Besides, I am none too vigorous myself, and that is what I have tried to express in the following lines, which you will surely remember henceforth (they *are* a little exaggerated):

> ... But you, the frailest of creatures,
> What can you do? What do you want?
> Is it your passion
> That will give you strength,
> Or staying at home
> To pamper yourself like this?

"And you can clearly see from these lines that I did want to leave... Although I admit that, in an even sadder fashion—even, let me say, discouraged—I added:

If you leave, then oh! beware! of . . . what?
And if you stay, the sickness is worse.
Death nips at your heels—now Death has come,
To carry you off without any further words.

"What comes next is about you, and it isn't finished. —But, if you insist . . . invite Barnaby instead!"

"Oh, you are so cruel this morning!" Angela said, and added: "He smells bad."

"Precisely, my dear Angela; big strong men always smell bad. —That is what my young friend Tancredo has tried to express in the following line:

Triumphant captains do smell terrible.

"(I can see you are thunderstruck: yes, I know, the meter.) —But, you're blushing! . . . And I was only trying to make you realize. —Ah, right! I also wanted to remark to you, my delicate friend, how serious I am when I'm joking around . . . Angela! I am frightfully weary! I am about to burst into tears.

"But first, let me dictate a few sentences; you write much faster than I do —plus I like to pace when I talk, it helps me. Here is a pencil and paper. Ah! sweet friend! how good that you've come! —Write, write as quick as you can; anyway, it is about our poor little trip:

". . . There are people who can be outside in an instant. Nature knocks upon their door, which opens out onto a vast plain, in which, no sooner have they stepped out, their place of residence is lost and forgotten. They find it again at night, when they need it to sleep in; they find it easily. They could, if they wanted, sleep beneath the stars, leave their home for a whole day—even forget it for longer. If you think this is natural, you have not understood what I mean. You should be more amazed by these things... As for us, I promise you that if we envy these people, who are so free, it is because every time we have built in sorrow a roof to shelter us, this roof has followed us everywhere, occupying the place above our heads from then on; it has kept us dry from the rain, true, but also blocked out the sun. We have slept in its shadow; worked, danced, embraced, thought in its shadow. Sometimes, when the splendors of the sunrise were sublime enough, we thought we might escape in the morning; we tried to forget it; we sneaked under the thatch roof like thieves, not trying to break in, but trying to break out—surreptitiously—and ran toward the plains. But the roof ran after us. It leaped after us like the bell in the old story that leaped after the people trying to avoid going to church. We never stopped feeling its weight on our heads. We had already carried all the material it took to construct it, when we were making it in the first place; now we could gauge the weight of the whole. It bowed our head, it stooped our shoulders—the way the weight of the Old Man of the Sea did Sinbad's.

"One never takes precautions at first; then, later, it's horrible. It is attached to us solely because of its weight. We cannot get free of it. Once you take up an idea, you have to carry it through to the end."

"Ah!" said Angela. "Unhappy, unhappy friend—why did you ever start *Marshlands*? when there are so many other subjects, more poetic ones too."

"Precisely, Angela! Write! Write! —(My God, could it be that today is the day I will finally be able to be sincere?)

"I don't understand in the least what you mean with this talk of more or less poetic. —All the anguish of a consumptive in a room that's too small, of a miner trying to climb back up into the daylight, of a pearl diver feeling on his head the weight of all the dark waves of the sea! All the sufferings of Plautus or Samson turning their mills, of Sisyphus rolling his rock; all the suffocation of a people enslaved—among others. All these oppressions I have known."

"You're dictating too fast," Angela said. "I can't keep up..."

"Then never mind! —Write no more, Angela, just listen! Listen—for my soul is in despair. How many times, oh how many times, have I made this gesture: after an awful nightmare, imagining the canopy of my bed becoming detached, falling down, wrapping round me, and weighing on my breast—I start up, after I awake, and stretch out my arms to push away from me some invisible walls—the gesture of pushing away someone whose impure breath I can feel too close to me—of holding back with outstretched arms the walls pressing in on me, always pressing in, or wobbling and tottering above our heads, massive, shaky; the same gesture as that of throwing off clothes which are too heavy, or cloaks off our shoulders. How many times, merely seeking a little fresh air, suffocating, have I known the gesture of opening the windows—and stopping myself, hopeless, because the one time when I did open them..."

"You caught a cold?" Angela said.

"...Because the one time when I did open them, I saw that they looked out onto backyards—out onto other low-ceilinged rooms—onto wretched yards, airless and sunless—and then, having seen this, I cried out in anguish with all of my strength: 'Lord! Lord! We are terribly shut in!'—and my voice echoed back to me at full volume, from the low ceiling. —Angela! Angela! What will we do now? Try once more to raise up these shrouds that oppress us? Or accustom ourselves to barely being able to breathe—so as to prolong our life in this tomb?"

"We have never been more alive," Angela said. "Tell me truly: Could anyone be more alive? What made you think that any greater vitality existed? Who told you it was possible? Hubert? Is he more alive for being so active?"

"Angela! Angela! Behold how I weep! Could it be that you have understood a little of my anguish? And your smile, can it be that I have finally put a little bitterness into it? — Wait! What? Now you're crying. —Good! I am happy! I act! —I am about to finish *Marshlands*!!"

Angela cried and cried, and her long hair came undone.

Then Hubert walked in. Seeing us disheveled, he said: "Sorry! I've come at a bad time," making as if to leave again.

His discretion moved me deeply, to the point where I cried: "Come in! Come in, my dear Hubert! It is never a bad time for us to see you!"—then added, sadly: "Don't you agree, Angela?"

She replied, "Yes, we were just having a little chat."

"I was passing by," Hubert said, "and I only have a few things to say. —I am leaving for Biskra the day after tomorrow. And I have convinced Roland to come with me."

Suddenly I was angry. "Presumptuous Hubert, it is I, *I*, who convinced Roland! The two of us were leaving Abel's— I remember it well—when I told him he should take that trip."

Hubert burst out laughing, and said: "You? But, my poor friend, just think—going as far as Montmorency was too much for you! How can you say... Anyway, maybe you were the first one to talk to him about it, but what is the use, I ask you, of putting ideas in people's heads? Do you think that that is where the decision to act is made?

"Please allow me to say here as well that you are strangely lacking in motive force ... You cannot give to others what you do not have. —Well, do you want to come with us? No? All right then! You see?

"So, my dear Angela, goodbye—I'll come to see you again."
He left.

"You can see, my complacent Angela," I said, "that I am staying with you ... But don't think it's out of love."

"Oh, no! I realize that," she replied.

"But, Angela, look!" I cried, with a glimmer of hope: "It's almost eleven! Oh! Now it's too late for church!"

Then she said with a sigh: "We will go to the four o'clock service."

And everything relapsed again.

Angela had to go.

Happening to catch sight of my daily planner, I saw the note there about visiting the impoverished family and gardener. I rushed to the post office and telegrammed:

"Hubert! Your destitute families!"

Then I went home to reread the *Petit Carême* sermons and await a response.

—At two o'clock, I received the wire. It said: "Crap. Letter follows."

—At which, sadness enveloped me still more completely.

"If Hubert leaves," I whimpered, "who will come see me at six o'clock? —Once *Marshlands* is finished, God only knows what I'll be able to do. Not poetry, not drama, I know that much ... I'm not very good at either one, and my aesthetic principles are entirely against conceiving a novel.

"I have already thought about taking up once more my old subject of POLDERLANDS—it would follow quite nicely from *Marshlands*, and not contradict what I've just done ..."

At three o'clock, a courier brought me Hubert's letter. It said: "I leave my five impoverished families in your care; a document is coming under separate cover which will give you their names and the necessary information. As for my various other businesses, I am entrusting them to Richard and his brother-in-law, you wouldn't understand the first thing about any of it. Goodbye—I'll write you from Biskra."

Then I opened my daily planner again and wrote on the Monday page: "Try to get up at six."

At three thirty I went to pick up Angela. We went to the service at l'Oratoire du Louvre together.

At five o'clock—I went to visit my poor. Then, as the weather grew cooler, I went home. I closed my windows and started to write ...

At six o'clock, my dear friend Gaspard walked in. He was back from fencing school. He said:

"So! Hard at work?"

I replied: "I am writing *Polderlands* ..."

. . . .

ENVOI

Oh! how the day took pains
This morning to wash the plains.

We played the pipe for you,
You didn't listen.

We sang
And you did not dance.

And then when we wanted to dance
There was no one playing the pipe.

So ever since our misfortúne,
I much prefer the lovely moon.

To the dogs it is sadness-bringing;
It sets the toad musicians singing.

In the deep of benevolent ponds
It silently, wordlessly expànds;

Too, its tepid nudity
Bleeds in perpetuity.

Toward our shepherd's hut we took
The flock with nary a shepherd's crook.

But it wanted to the festivities to be brought
Which would make all our prophecies come to nought.

The white flocks were led, as though to water,
But actually to the slaughter.

And we have built on sand
Cathedrals ephemeral if grand.

VARIANT

OR TO GO once more, O forest full of mystery? To go to the place I know well, where in water dead and dark the leaves of bygone years, of lovely springtimes, steep and soften still.

There rest best my useless resolutions; there, in the end, my thoughts diminish to essentially nothing.

TABLE OF THE MOST REMARKABLE SENTENCES IN *MARSHLANDS*

*Given the prevalence of personal preferences, we leave the job of completing this page to each individual reader.

APPENDIX

1. Two Poems

MY OLD *subject of POLDERLANDS* (p. 84). The French title is *Polders*, a near anagram of *Paludes*. Polders, or tracts of reclaimed wetlands especially common in the Netherlands, are indeed a suitable subject to follow marshlands. Like the narrator, Gide had taken up the subject before: Poem XVII in Gide's first book, *The Notebooks and Poetry of André Walter* (1890), is also called "*Polders*"; the twentieth and last poem in the book is paludal as well.

POLDERLANDS

A little lamb explores
The miserable moors.

A gray sky; green silt
And verdigris grass;
Abandoned ewes graze past
Along iridescent streams.

A sun drained of color,
Level with the withered horizon;
Our sadness melts into tears
Along tracks it has not been taught.

Somnolent water drains away,
Strains to listen. A lamb
Lifts its head from nibbling grass
Between the banks of green silt . . .

XX

More monotonous plains, marshy and trackless; they extend between the hills. Rushes and underbrush. Wandering all the way to what the twilight brings to an end . . .

Suddenly, bells toll. Lights can be seen running along the hills—snatches of organ music in the lit church, chants from afar.

Then you tell me: "We have to hurry." But our lamps are too weak, they have gone out, we walk in darkness. Our tired feet get caught in the bushes.

. . . All this to get to a closed door: that of the giant church. And no one sees us, for our lamps are out.

On the stairs, in tears, we hear the organ music and voices, gushing out from under the door. Light from the windows pours out into the night.

Maybe this is all just a dream
And we are about to wake.

You tell me:
"I think we are living in someone else's dream
And that is why we are so passive."
It can't go on like this forever.

"I think we had better try
To fall back asleep."

2. Three Scenes Appearing Only in the First and Second Editions

[BALDAKIN DESCRIBES HIS BOOK]
(p. 46, after "Now I can breathe!")

THEN I heard a voice in my ear: "As for me—I am writing *Briareus*."

It was Baldakin, mainly a journalist.

I said: "Ah! *Briareus*!"

"Yes, the hundred-armed man," he said. "Briareus the giant. —And do you know who Briareus is?"

"???"

"Well, he is The People."

"You amaze me. Really?!"

"You will see what I mean in a moment. The giant's hundred hands, his hundred feet, each possesses an individual consciousness, they have to; the giant's one brain can possess only common sense. Do you see what I mean?"

"Not quite yet."

"Listen. No hand, no foot, can have any immediate sensation of the pains or delights of its ninety-nine confreres. Every hand longs to be warm, so it burrows into embers. Briareus, with his crude small brain, cannot feel every hand individually, all that reaches him is the end result of the hundred different sensations. He is a stupid brute and has not yet conceived of justice. A certain parity is enough for him. If one of his hands is too hot, he sticks a different hand in ice. That does a good enough job of giving him the pleasure he would feel from a hundred moderately warm hands; he has other hands in the embers, he loves it. Besides, a hot hand is stronger, it won't let go of anything... So! Now do you understand Briareus?

"And you see why Briareus, the People, will never be happy? Because he can't do with everything what he does with his hundred moderately warm hands..." Leaning toward me, he added under his breath: "He would need a hundred women, you understand—it's impossible—and he would have to enjoy them all together, otherwise he would never achieve complete pleasure."

"That seems to contradict somewhat what you said first," I insinuated.

"Actually it doesn't. —And now perhaps you will ask me why every hand, offending and thus cut off by auto-amputation, cannot escape the larger body that wants to plunge it into ice? Your remark is excellent, I see we understand each other. —But wait: every organ of every body has a tendency to become a complete organism, you know. If it is detached prematurely from the larger torso, it dies. If not, the hands live free. Hands, escape from the ice!

"The good thing is that Briareus, once those are no longer compensating for the heat of the others, will suddenly start to feel a burning in his feet that are by the fire.—Quick! Other hands into the ice! And so the story continues.

"Do you see what I mean, Poet? —Now tell me the story of *Marshlands*."

"*Marshlands*," I began, "is the story of a detached hand."

"Hah! Hah!" he exclaimed. "The hot hand!"

"Not at all. The warm hand."

"Didn't you understand anything I said?..."

"Of course I did."

"So why warm?"

"How should I know? —that is its state. Surely you don't think that every detached hand rises at once into the heavens? Mine detaches into an enormous marsh of lukewarm water. You can see no end to it." And, leaning toward him, I said in a very low voice, to be polite: "The marsh is right here. We are in it!"

"I'm not sure I follow you," he said.

"Be patient, you'll see. Detach the hands from Briareus, and they will link up with one another using all of their fingers."

"No they won't."

"Please, allow me to continue. Surely you don't think that your hand can only be attached to a torso? They are connected by all the prison chains, by all their fingers to all the other fingers, through all their pores to the air: they belong to everything, at the right time and place, and the time is a gray and overcast day, and the place is the marshland."

"All right, I see, the time, the place, fine, but not connected to everything."

"Please allow me to continue," I said. "Are you detached?"

"Yes, at least I hope so."

The conversation had made us sweat; I wanted to show him that there was no way to open a window for us, because the others would catch cold. That is, I wanted to cleverly suggest it to him. So, taking a handkerchief out of my pocket, I subtly insinuated: "Don't you think it's stifling hot in here?!"

He took out his handkerchief too, mopped his brow, then replied, suddenly calm: "No, not at all..."

[STANISLAUS SPEAKS]
(p. 47, after "then we wouldn't be able to hear each other")

Just then, voices could be heard from the living room: "Shh! Shh!! Stanislaus is going to say something."

He had already started to speak. Everyone else fell silent. Stanislaus said: "...You are trying to sow seeds in soil not yet sufficiently tilled. You think our work is destructive, because you are looking at it in and of itself, but it cannot be considered in isolation from its consequences. It may sometimes be the case that the same man works the field and sows the seed, but at least he does not do these two things at the same time, and we usually find that the succession is not so rapid: one generation labors for another to plant; a third can take pride in a crop from the earth; still another then reaps the harvest. Some make bread from the wheat, while others will eat it.

"Work gives people an appetite, but those who hunger are not those who eat; the hunger of the fathers is satisfied only in the children. That is what makes us want to create these children, and makes us love them—as though, from their dreams of a full belly, we might finally have a life more full; as though the thought of their future food could satisfy us!"

"Ah! Bravo, bravo!" came the cries from all sides.

"We are a generation of laborers! Dying of hunger from our work, and with no other comfort than the rotten remains of past sustenance, canned food, leftover casserole! Or, worse: things already eaten!

"Let us labor before the frost comes. Who knows, who knows where our grandchildren will go to find seeds to plant?—For now, our fields are bleak. If only a rain from heaven would come to water them..."

Excited by his talk of bleak fields, and thinking I might have a talk with him, I sprung at his hand, hoping to shake it, and said: "Ah! Sir!..."

But he, perspiring with effort, quickly raised his handkerchief to his brow, hoping to avoid my handshake, and said: "I don't like writers. They neither harvest nor labor nor sow, and they content themselves with casserole."

"Oh! Sir," I began. "Surely I, who..."

[THE NARRATOR IN A MALLARMÉAN MOMENT]
(p. 62, after "works for me on normal days")

Still, as I habitually do, I copied the following note onto a page for December, for I was curious to see if my will would persevere and if Magloire would too. If he didn't, I would have been right to do nothing after all.

Today I will do nothing; I will wait to take the trip. I don't want to go visit anyone—too bad—I'm leaving—I don't have to *take care of* things anymore. And I can't stand it when people ask me how long I'll be gone—because, in the end, it is precisely because I won't be gone long that I can leave like this, without the proper preparations. I don't want anyone to come visit me: Alcides was bad enough. If I weren't looking forward to my trip like this, I would have been polite to him; at least I maintain that I probably would have been; he might have had breakfast here, and toward the end of the meal I would have told him the story of *Marshlands*, and he would not have understood it very well. —Let me insist: If no one else were around I would never criticize either them or myself, it is once I see them that I immediately become critical. I insist, I insist: to partake, come what may, of the deliciousness of being alone at the moment I finish my meal—to wait, ringed round by my books, Darwin, Bentham, Malte-Brun, and the one desiring me most welcomingly of all to take it down, my Virgil.

...*"Ego ubi tempus erit, omnis in fonte lavabo."*

3. *Afterword to the New Edition of* Marshlands

"A YOUNG man full of passion," as [Chateaubriand's] René says—burning and chaste, after a year of travel, during which, by choice but not without difficult struggles, he was able to banish books for a long time, raise the curtains, open the windows, and shatter the grimy windowpanes: everything that comes between us and the Other, making nature flat and dull; for he thought it was better to marvel at nature, let his resolute joie de vivre and need to see every thing as it truly is keep him busy—was finally able to bring his life and his thoughts into harmony, in accord with the wild optimism to which he had been led first by his temperament, then by his admiration for Goethe and patient consideration of Leibniz. Sick for almost a year, he desolately desperately loved the light, which made him happier, or so he thought, than anything had ever made him before, even study.

Among a deep-rooted people with a different religion and different morality, sometimes contrary to ours and yet beautiful, he was suddenly able to see his own analytic habits and need to argue and convince as very strange, in fact pathological, now that he thought back on it. Up until then it had often plagued him, this restlessness of men of the North who always take the better as the enemy of the good. Suddenly, he had almost no further need to understand anything, seeing thought as an unnecessary perplexity, admiration as a sufficient prayer. He gladly said, like Luther to the troubled young theologian, "Go and drink!" From there he thought back to Paris—that restless agitation while staying in place, that localization of happiness, that myopia of windows, controls on pleasure, interception of the sun, stifling of people who insist on never breathing air except through their cigarettes. He had certainly been far away, and for a long time too, to think of these things with such a smile, for he lacked the confrontational spirit and laughed at nothing but what he had known himself.

Never mind. He wrote a book, and since he felt like laughing he took it all to be equally ludicrous: he who exerted control, he who tried to evade it, he who did not know how to escape, and the control itself. He decided, let it be said in passing, that there were two simple solutions: either to ignore the controls (avoid them, eliminate them), or not to perceive them in the first place. The author wrote this book, and, as a way to laugh all the more, to show that he was not laughing only at others, he wrote it *in the first person.*

"It's a memoir," people immediately thought, and in fact his earlier books had announced as much. The intellectual and spiritual vices he is invoking here, in order to laugh at them: "They are his own!" And even though the book, confessional as it might be, contradicted his earlier books, someone said: "You are so sad!"

Not in the least, I couldn't be happier!

Someone else: "Ah! You are so psychological!"

I loathe psychology.

"But then what are you trying to say?"

That's just my point: one can't say anything.

"You must be terribly bored!"

Not me, never.

"Your book is too full of symbols."

That's to make fun of symbols.

"The air is not always gray! There are nice days too!"

What do you mean *too*? All my days are nice! Believe me: I am not the nameless person who says "I" in *Marshlands*. I have no complaints about anything—not even myself. I consider myself content. Happily, I am happy. What I laugh at is *Marshlands*—I wrote it to laugh at it . . . Oh these endless protestations!—Maybe I should have written at the end of my book, as I'd originally wanted to: "For those who could not understand it, for those who didn't understand me, for myself, for everyone"? An artificial book requires an equally artificial conclusion.

But let the patient reader regard the whole book as nothing but a preface to the one he will soon be able to enjoy reading, called *Les Nourritures terrestres—The Fruits of the Earth*.

"Awful title," Angela said.

"I'm sorry you think so," I replied.

Truly, it is a terrible thing to make a book; as you well know, dear reader, for you make them too. And of all the intellectual compulsions in the world, one of the most annoying is the inability of readers to simply accept every sentence as it is given to him. He takes seriously the page on which you are joking, and when you are speaking in earnest he gives a subtle smile and says: "I can see that you are joking!" With these judgments, the past jeopardizes the future. They do not admit that we are an indefinite mix of laughter and melancholy, like a partly cloudy day. Having cried just once, our laughter is not believed; having joked just once, we are no longer taken seriously. Every book has to defend itself anew; no sooner is it born than the book must surround itself with protections, objections, refutations, like the infant Hercules in swaddling clothes and strangled snakes. No one seems to understand that, having done a thing, what one wants is precisely to do something else. And yet the first thing imposes an obligation: people now expect the same, dressed up slightly differently. Specializations and relapses! The passing of time proposes, habit imposes, the public applauds.

Oh, ye world endlessly reborn! Who can perceive your immortal sameness, beneath your various everchanging surface? Oh, Nature, always like everything and like yourself! Who, who will ever have enough of the new forms in your monotony, the inexhaustible energy of your laughter and your harmonies—source of the inexhaustible supply of love that I love! Everything comic, born of a sense of mismatch—every newly perceived harmony—permits and promises a new burst of laughter. The comedy develops together with the sense of harmony. *The Voyage of Urien* [1893] enabled me to laugh in *Marshlands*, while *Marshlands* makes it possible for me to be serious today.

For having created a "Table of the Most Remarkable Sentences in *Marshlands*" (and how I smiled as I did so!), I was thought to have been making fun of the reader. Who thought this? —A reader!

Too bad for him; I only wanted to laugh with him, and at myself: one can laugh only at oneself, a self that is surely funny enough, but one never notices. The joke is always on the joker, never on what is being made fun of. Mockery is always a profanation. Anyone who thinks he sees something dull and ordinary in this world is wrong: there is nothing the least bit dull and ordinary in it, and that which you initially believe to be so is only being squeezed together by the rest, and it often gains in depth as a result. If it looks dull to you, then it is you who are looking at it too close up; step back! Enlarge your vision; do not artificially isolate something so that it appears ordinary. —The ordinary exists only in the works of man, and only works of art cannot be excused for being ordinary, because their beauty alone motivates and justifies them—and because they are *self-contained*.

I am not Tityrus! Nothing in life seems ordinary to me. I could have preserved my reputation if I had told you up front: "*Marshlands* is the story of a defective spirit!" —His flaws? Just one is enough: He prefers the better to the good. That is why he want to improve everyone else. Spiritual flaws—Christian virtues—let me not insist on the point, for that would be to say what? I am not joking about anything. The fact remains that Tityrus always has everything he needs in order to do nothing. To do something, you need less than you need in order to *no longer* do anything.

In that "Table of the Most Remarkable Sentences," I wanted to show anyone who had not yet understood me what mattered most to me in the book, by brutally boiling it down to two sentences. Hubert says to the narrator: "So! Hard at work?" He says it with astonishment. He even repeats it. I reply: "I am writing *Marshlands*." —Just like that, an idea is taken up. "Once you take up an idea, you have to carry it through to the end." —And there you have the subject of my book. *Marshlands* is the story of an idea, more than of anything else; it is the story of the spiritual malaise that that idea causes. Is an idea an aspect of life? No, it is part of a fever, part of a semblance of life. It is a succubus, feeding on us, while we exist merely to give *it* life. I could have made any other idea my subject in a book like this, it wouldn't matter.

People think of ideas as too much like dead things, subject to logic; actually they are alive. They live at our expense, in our brains. However they might glow with life, they are like floating algae, which looks faded, never the same, when it's taken out of the water—and yet in the water it is interesting: vital, moving, full of life, restless. What is an idea like? It is like a cancerous bacteria that I put into a child's brain; it doesn't grow, I assume, or if it does, it will be directly from the child's brain: that is where it will put down roots, permeate it with sickness, suck out the child's health for its own parasitic life. *We are irrevocably given over to the idea.*

What else is an idea like? It is like the little grain of wheat described in the Gospels. It is the smallest of seeds—but when it grows, as grow it must, it surpasses the giant trees of the earth, and the birds of the sky come live in its branches. The idea is like the Kingdom of God, about which John also says: It must increase, but I must decrease. We cannot avoid it: one does not escape from God; God possesses us without end. So let us consecrate ourselves to the idea.

Moreover, I like every book to include its own refutation, but hidden. It should not sit atop its idea, afraid to look it in the face. I like it to include what denies it, to self-destruct. It should be so entirely self-contained that it is impossible to destroy any of it without destroying the whole, leaving nothing behind, no residue, no ashes, not a scrap; it should be like those chemical compounds, agglomerations, juxtapositions of equipotences so perfect that they stay calmly in equilibrium until a more ardent spark comes along that can reduce it in an instant, annihilate it, at least to our eyes, into a volatile disappearance, a subtilized gas. —A laughing gas.

The world, it seems to me, is only that, nothing less than that. —What am I saying? —Better: It is a whole only in that way.

I said all these things and many more in *Marshlands*; but you understood nothing—as I explained in *Marshlands* itself. For today, one has to either scream as though at the deaf or risk not being heard—but that is a false choice. The work of art is reluctant to scream that way. Not to be heard is like speaking in the wilderness; even if it blossom in the desert, I am on the side of the work of art.

Let me add one more thing: *Marshlands* is the story of someone who does not understand life, who writhes and worries for having believed in anything except the *one thing needful.*

Summer 1895

4. *From* Prometheus Misbound *(1899)*

THE STORY OF TITYRUS
(as told by Prometheus in Paris)

I

IN THE beginning was Tityrus.

And Tityrus, alone, grew bored, surrounded on all sides as he was by marshland.

Now it happened that Menalcas passed by, and he planted both an idea in Tityrus's head and a seed in the marsh that Tityrus saw before him. And this idea was the seed, and this seed was the Idea. And with God's help, the seed sprouted and grew into a little plant, and Tityrus, morning noon and night, knelt down before it and thanked God for having given it to him. And the plant grew. Since its roots were powerful, it soon drew all the water from the soil around it, so Tityrus had firm ground on which to set his feet, rest his head, and fortify the work of his hands.

When this plant had grown as tall as Tityrus himself, he could take a certain pleasure in sleeping outstretched in its shadow. Now, this sapling, being an oak, was fated to grow to enormous size; it grew so large that before long the work of Tityrus's hands no longer sufficed to weed and hoe the soil around it, water it, prune it, massage it, trim it, clear the caterpillars from it, and ensure that its fruits, both various and numerous, were gathered in at the proper season. And so he called unto himself a weeder, a hoer, a waterer, a pruner, a masseur, a trimmer, a caterpillar-clearer, and some boys to gather fruit. And since each had to stick strictly to his respective specialty, there was a good chance that the tasks would be performed well.

They all needed to be paid, and Tityrus, to keep track of the payments, needed a bookkeeper, who soon shared with a cashier the job of tending to Tityrus's fortune, which increased as the oak.

Certain conflicts having arisen between the pruner and the trimmer concerning the proper apportionment of their respective functions, Tityrus grasped the need for an arbitrator, flanked by a brace of lawyers, one pro and one contra; he hired a secretary to take down their judgments, and, since the only reason to take them down was to refer to them in future, an archivist as well. Little by little, houses rose up from the ground; there had to be police on the streets, and officers to prevent any abuses.

Overwhelmed with work, Tityrus fell ill; he sent for a doctor, who advised him to take a wife. And since Tityrus alone was not enough for all of these people, he was forced to choose a deputy, who then had Tityrus elected mayor. From that moment on, he had all too little free time to cast a line and fish from the windows of his house, which still, as before, opened onto the marshes.

Then Tityrus instituted holidays for his people's pleasure; but since these festivities were expensive, and none of the people had enough money, Tityrus began to levy a tax on each so that he could lend to all.

Now, the oak, in the middle of the plain (for in spite of the city, in spite of the efforts of all these men, it had never stopped being the plain)—this oak, I say, in the middle of the plain, had no trouble being situated in such a way that one of its sides was in shadow, the other in the sun. Under this oak, then, Tityrus dispensed justice on the shady side and answered the call of nature on the sunny side.

And Tityrus was happy, for he felt that his life was both useful to others and excessively busy.

II

Human effort can be cultivated. This fostering of Tityrus's activity only seemed to increase it; his natural ingenuity suggesting all sorts of other employments to him, he was soon to be seen hard at work furnishing, carpeting, and arranging his home. The wall hangings were displayed properly; every object was admirably well suited to its purpose. Being industrious, he was an excellent empiricist: he even invented a little acrostic hook rack for hanging his sponges on the wall, which, after four days, he no longer found suitable at all

And Tityrus had a room built next to his own, for the interests of the nation. The two rooms shared an entrance, in an attempt to suggest that his interests and the nation's were the same, but, since the common entrance circulated the same air into both rooms, the two fireplaces could not both draw at the same time, and in cold weather, when a fire was lit in the one, smoke filled the other. Thus Tityrus got into the habit of opening his window on days when he wanted to light a fire.

Since Tityrus protected everything and worked to promote

the propagation of various species, the time soon came when slugs crawled along his garden paths in such abundance that he could not put his foot down without fear of squashing one, and he ended up resigning himself to going out less often.

He set up a circulating library, with a librarian, from whom he took out a subscription. And, since her name was Angela, he got into the habit of going to spend the evening with her every third day. This was how Tityrus learned metaphysics, algebra, and theodicy. Together, Tityrus and Angela began to cultivate various pleasant artistic capacities, with no little success. When Angela revealed a particular taste for music, they rented a grand piano, on which Angela would execute the little melodies he would compose for her between visits.

Tityrus said to her: "All this work is killing me. I can't go on. I feel all worn out. All these solidarities activate my scruples: when they increase, I decrease. What can I do?"

"What if we went away?" Angela said to him.

"I cannot: I have my oak tree."

"What if you abandoned it," Angela said.

"Abandon my oak tree! What are you thinking?"

"Isn't it big enough to grow on its own?"

"But I am attached to it."

"So detach," Angela replied.

And not long afterward, realizing that, all in all, his work, his responsibilities, his various scruples, and even the oak tree were not enough to keep him there, Tityrus smiled, set his sail to the wind, and departed, bringing along the cash box and Angela. As that day came to an end, the two of them walked down the boulevard leading from the Madeleine to the Opéra.

III

The boulevard that evening had an unusual appearance. Something strange and ceremonial seemed about to happen. An enormous crowd, serious, nervous, was rushing around, blocking the sidewalk and almost spilling out onto the street, which a line of Paris policemen were having great difficulty keeping clear. The outdoor seating areas in front of the restaurants, disproportionally enlarged with the deployment of extra tables and chairs, only made the obstruction more complete to the point where it was impossible to move. Now and then an impatient spectator jumped up onto his chair for a moment, just long enough for someone to ask him to sit back down. Clearly, everyone was waiting for something; there was no question but that something was about to come down the street between the banks of the sidewalks and lines of guards.

Angela and Tityrus, having found a table with great difficulty and rented it for an enormous amount of money, sat down with two glasses of beer in front of them and asked the waiter: "What is everyone waiting for?"

"Where has Monsieur been? Does Monsieur not know that we are awaiting Meliboeus? He's supposed to come by between five and six . . . and wait. Listen! I think I hear his flute."

A faint sound of reed pipes wafted over from down the boulevard. The crowd waited still more eagerly, shuddering even. The sound grew louder and came closer.

"Oh it's so moving!" Angela said.

The setting sun sent its rays shooting from one end of the boulevard to the other. Then at last Meliboeus could be seen approaching, as if emerging from the splendors of the sunset, preceded by the simple sound of his flute.

At first, they could make out only his general appearance, but when he came closer, Angela said: "Oh! He's so lovely!"

Melibœus, meanwhile, having reached where Tityrus was, ceased to play his song on the flute, stopped abruptly, saw Angela, and everyone noticed that he was naked.

"Oh!" said Angela, leaning toward Tityrus, "he's so handsome! His midriff is so fit! His pipes are so alluring!"

Tityrus was a little embarrassed.

"Ask him where he's going!" Angela said.

"Where are you going?" Tityrus inquired.

"*Eo Romam*," Melibœus replied.

"What did he say?" Angela asked.

Tityrus: "You wouldn't understand, darling."

"But you can explain it to me," Angela said

"*Romam*," Melibœus repeated. "*Urbem quam dicunt Romam.*"

Angela: "Oh! It's so delicious, what he's saying! What does it mean?"

Tityrus: "I assure you, my dear Angela, it is not as delicious as all that. It simply means that he's going to Rome."

"Rome!" Angela said dreamily. "Oh, how I'd love to see Rome!"

Melibœus, taking up his reed pipes once more, struck up again his primitive tune. At the sound of it, Angela excitedly sat up, stood up, went over, took the elbow Melibœus had crooked for her, and the two of them continued like that down the boulevard, receded, dissolved, disappeared in the definitive twilight.

The crowd, now unleashed, burst into a tumult. Questions were heard from all sides: "What did he say?" —"What did he do?" —"Who was that woman?" A few moments later, when the evening papers appeared, a ferocious curiosity snatched every copy away like a tornado. Suddenly everyone learned that this woman was Angela, and that this Melibœus fellow was a naked man on his way to Italy.

All curiosity sated, the crowd flowed off like running water, leaving the boulevards empty. —And Tityrus found himself alone once more, completely surrounded by the marsh.

NOTES ON THE LATIN IN *MARSHLANDS* AND MARTIN'S MENU

MANY OF these notes are adapted from the Pléiade edition.

5   *Dic cur hic.* "Explain yourself." Literally: Say why [you're] here, what your purpose in life is; say why you're doing this, why here and now. A medieval proverb, common among humanists, e.g., Johann Michael Moscherosch (1601–1669).

10 *Et tibi magna satis quamvis lapis omnia nudus / Limosoque palus obducat pascua junco.* "And large enough to satisfy you, though bare rock and a marsh of muddy rushes cover all your pastures" (Virgil, *Eclogues* I.48–49, Melibœus to Tityrus about the latter's fields). The word *palus* here, "marsh," is the singular of *Paludes,* the Latin word that is the title of Gide's novel; in French, *paludes* is a neologism, though there is an adjective, *paludéen,* meaning "paludal."

24 *similia similibus.* "Like unto like." *Similia similibus curantur* or *curentur* is the law of similars: "Like cures like" (Paracelsus); "Let like be used to cure like" (the basic principle of homeopathic medicine).

31 *nigra sed formosa.* "Black but comely" (Song of Solomon 1:5).

41 *Numero deus impare gaudet.* "God delights in odd numbers" (Virgil, *Eclogues* VIII.75); that is, odd numbers

are lucky. The French translation offered in the original text is more cognate than I could manage in English: *Numéro deux se réjouit d'être impair* ("The number two is delighted to be odd").

41 *Et dona ferentes.* "[Beware of Greeks] bearing gifts" (Virgil, *Aenead* II.49).

44 *Tityre recubans.* "Tityrus, lying down" (Virgil, *Eclogues* I.1).

46 *Et tibi magna satis.* "And large enough to satisfy you" (see note to page 10).

47 *velle non discitur.* As Barnaby the moralist paraphrases: "The will cannot be taught" (Seneca, quoted by Schopenhauer).

50 *recubans.* "Lying down" (see note to page 44).

62 *Tityre semper recubans.* "Tityrus, always lying down" (not a quote).

98 *Ego ubi tempus erit, omnis in fonte lavabo.* "[Tityrus, keep the browsing goats away from the streams:] I will wash them all in a spring when the time is right" (Virgil, *Eclogues* III.97, spoken by Damœtas).

111 *Eo Romam.* "I am going to Rome" (textbook Latin sentence).

111 *Urbem quam dicunt Romam.* "To the city they call Rome" (Virgil, *Eclogues* I.19: Tityrus to Melibœus).

A conclave of symbolists inspired the respective courses of Martin's paradigmatic menu (p. 42):

Joris-Karl Huysmans (1848–1907), author of *À rebours* (*Against Nature,* 1884), the great Symbolist novel. The association between Huysmans and soup may be pure coincidence, but it should perhaps be noted that Paul Verlaine's poem "The Evening Soup" (1884) is dedicated to Huysmans.

Maurice Barrès (1862–1923) introduced Gide to Mallarmé and the symbolist clique. "Le Banquet," the title of this chapter, refers to Plato's *Symposium* (known as *Le Banquet* in French), but also recalls a banquet organized by Barrès and hosted by Mallarmé on February 2, 1891, to which Barrès brought Gide. (On the landing of Mallarmé's apartment, where Mallarmé also hosted his famous *mardis* or Tuesday salons, there was in fact a bench, like the one on which Martin and the narrator are sitting.) Later in *Marshlands*, Barrès is referred to as "a politician": he was a Decadent writer, notably of the trilogy *The Cult of the Self*, whose first two volumes Gide particularly admired, but had also been elected in 1889 to the Chamber of Deputies, the start of a long conservative political career. With regard to steak: "For us other analysts, he thought, nothing that happens within escapes us. I distinctly see the little morsels of beef, red and monstrous, battling in my digestive tract" (*Under Barbarian Eyes*, the first volume in Barrès's trilogy).

Gabriel Trarieux (1870–1940), poet and playwright at whose house Gide met Marcel Proust on May 1, 1891. No known connection to selected vegetables.

Stéphane Mallarmé (1842–1898), greatest symbolist poet and a literary and spiritual hero of Gide's. The line of Mallarmé's misquoted to Angela later in the book actually is a slightly misquoted line of Mallarmé's, from the poem "Sea Breeze." Gide gave Mallarmé Copy A of the first printing of *Marshlands*, receiving in return a letter of convoluted Mallarméan praise: "The precious, acidic drops of irony these hundred pages hold: a unique quintessence. . . . This spirited affabulation well-nigh a miracle.... It is good, or perhaps genius: this discreet, terrible bantering with the flower of the soul. Thank you for the affecting honor of including my name."

Chartreuse certainly tastes symbolist enough. The real liqueur comes in two varieties, green and yellow, while the Wildean "golden-green" is a strangely ambiguous sort, especially since Gide makes the adjective masculine while the noun is feminine (*Chartreuse vert doré*). Oscar Wilde (1854–1900) needs no introduction; Gide met him and fell under his spell in late 1891, and saw him again in Florence in spring 1894, while traveling from Algeria, where he had begun *Marshlands*, to Switzerland, where he would finish it. Early in 1895, Gide found himself in Algeria with Wilde; according to Gide's autobiography, a homosexual experience he had there, arranged by Wilde, was decisive in his life. Gide closely followed the events of Wilde's trial and two-year imprisonment (1895–97). *Marshlands* was finished in late 1894 and published in the spring of 1895.

OTHER NEW YORK REVIEW CLASSICS

For a complete list of titles, visit www.nyrb.com or write to:
Catalog Requests, NYRB, 435 Hudson Street, New York, NY 10014

J.R. ACKERLEY My Dog Tulip
J.R. ACKERLEY My Father and Myself
J.R. ACKERLEY We Think the World of You
HENRY ADAMS The Jeffersonian Transformation
RENATA ADLER Pitch Dark
RENATA ADLER Speedboat
AESCHYLUS Prometheus Bound; translated by Joel Agee
ROBERT AICKMAN Compulsory Games
LEOPOLDO ALAS His Only Son *with* Doña Berta
CÉLESTE ALBARET Monsieur Proust
DANTE ALIGHIERI The Inferno
KINGSLEY AMIS The Alteration
KINGSLEY AMIS Ending Up
KINGSLEY AMIS Girl, 20
KINGSLEY AMIS The Green Man
KINGSLEY AMIS Lucky Jim
KINGSLEY AMIS The Old Devils
KINGSLEY AMIS Take a Girl Like You
ROBERTO ARLT The Seven Madmen
U.R. ANANTHAMURTHY Samskara: A Rite for a Dead Man
IVO ANDRIĆ Omer Pasha Latas
WILLIAM ATTAWAY Blood on the Forge
W.H. AUDEN (EDITOR) The Living Thoughts of Kierkegaard
W.H. AUDEN W. H. Auden's Book of Light Verse
ERICH AUERBACH Dante: Poet of the Secular World
EVE BABITZ Eve's Hollywood
EVE BABITZ I Used to Be Charming: The Rest of Eve Babitz
EVE BABITZ Slow Days, Fast Company: The World, the Flesh, and L.A.
DOROTHY BAKER Cassandra at the Wedding
DOROTHY BAKER Young Man with a Horn
J.A. BAKER The Peregrine
S. JOSEPHINE BAKER Fighting for Life
HONORÉ DE BALZAC The Human Comedy: Selected Stories
HONORÉ DE BALZAC The Memoirs of Two Young Wives
HONORÉ DE BALZAC The Unknown Masterpiece *and* Gambara
VICKI BAUM Grand Hotel
SYBILLE BEDFORD A Favorite of the Gods *and* A Compass Error
SYBILLE BEDFORD A Legacy
SYBILLE BEDFORD A Visit to Don Otavio: A Mexican Journey
MAX BEERBOHM The Prince of Minor Writers: The Selected Essays of Max Beerbohm
MAX BEERBOHM Seven Men
STEPHEN BENATAR Wish Her Safe at Home
FRANS G. BENGTSSON The Long Ships
WALTER BENJAMIN The Storyteller Essays
ALEXANDER BERKMAN Prison Memoirs of an Anarchist
GEORGES BERNANOS Mouchette
MIRON BIAŁOSZEWSKI A Memoir of the Warsaw Uprising
ADOLFO BIOY CASARES Asleep in the Sun
PAUL BLACKBURN (TRANSLATOR) Proensa
CAROLINE BLACKWOOD Great Granny Webster